BIAS IN AMERICA

LGBTQ IN AMERICA

Barbara Sheen

San Diego, CA

© 2021 ReferencePoint Press, Inc.
Printed in the United States

For more information, contact:
ReferencePoint Press, Inc.
PO Box 27779
San Diego, CA 92198
www.ReferencePointPress.com

ALL RIGHTS RESERVED.
No part of this work covered by the copyright hereon may be reproduced or used in any form or by any means—graphic, electronic, or mechanical, including photocopying, recording, taping, web distribution, or information storage retrieval systems—without the written permission of the publisher.

LIBRARY OF CONGRESS CATALOGING-IN-PUBLICATION DATA

Names: Sheen, Barbara, author.
Title: LGBTQ in America / Barbara Sheen.
Description: San Diego : ReferencePoint Press, 2020. | Series: Bias in America | Includes bibliographical references and index.
Identifiers: LCCN 2020017077 (print) | LCCN 2020017078 (ebook) | ISBN 9781682828977 (library binding) | ISBN 9781682828984 (ebook)
Subjects: LCSH: Sexual minorities--United States--Juvenile literature. | Sexual minorities--Legal status, laws, etc.--United States. | Human rights--United States--Juvenile literature. | Gay rights--United States--Juvenile literature.
Classification: LCC HQ73.3.U6 S44 2020 (print) | LCC HQ73.3.U6 (ebook) | DDC 306.760973--dc23
LC record available at https://lccn.loc.gov/2020017077
LC ebook record available at https://lccn.loc.gov/2020017078

CONTENTS

Introduction   4
Many Challenges

Chapter One   8
A Troubling History

Chapter Two   20
Growing Up LGBTQ Is Not Easy

Chapter Three   32
The Long Reach of Discrimination

Chapter Four   43
Violence and Hate Crimes

Chapter Five   54
What the Future Holds

Source Notes	65
Organizations and Websites	69
For Further Research	71
Index	73
Picture Credits	79
About the Author	80

INTRODUCTION

Many Challenges

Jordan is a young gay man who grew up in a conservative community where many residents are intolerant of LGBTQ people. As an adolescent, he felt different from his peers. He found himself more romantically attracted to boys than to girls. He suspected that he was gay, but fearing that others would reject him if he came out (disclosed his sexual orientation), he tried to deny his feelings. His classmates, however, sensed that he was different and harassed him. They called him homophobic slurs and generally made his life miserable. He recalls, "People were really mean. . . . I would walk down the hallway and people would look at me and whisper. I felt like an alien."[1]

Things outside of school were also difficult. Jordan's family members are conservative Christians. They, along with Jordan and most members of the community, faithfully attended a church whose doctrine regarded homosexuals as sinners who are punished in the afterlife. This doctrine frightened Jordan. He prayed fervently that he would become straight. But his sexual orientation did not change, and eventually he came to accept who he was.

Jordan's parents, however, were not accepting. When Jordan came out to them, they rejected him. Because he was tired of denying who he was and was able to support himself, Jordan left home. He moved to a more tolerant and diverse city, met other members of the LGBTQ community, and found support and acceptance among them. "All my life I have been scared, fearful of being judged. I thought no one would ever accept me," he admits. "All my life I have been looking for acceptance, but . . . when I decided to be my own person . . . acceptance found me. . . . I am gay and I am happy and I am proud of myself."[2]

A Large and Diverse Group

Jordan is one of many Americans who identify as LGBTQ. According to a recent Gallup poll, more than 11 million adults, or 4.5 percent of the total US population, identify as LGBTQ. More than 8 million of these individuals are millennials. In the last decade, as Americans have become more accepting of the LGBTQ community, more young people have become open about their own status. However, since some individuals are reluctant to reveal their sexual orientation or gender identity due to the bias they might face, the total number of LGBTQ Americans may actually be greater.

> "I am gay and I am happy and I am proud of myself."[2]
>
> —Jordan, a gay man

The LGBTQ community is not only large but also diverse. It comprises people of varied ages, ethnicities, religions, and economic levels who identify with a particular sexual orientation or gender identity and share similar struggles for acceptance. The abbreviation *LGBTQ* is an umbrella term used to describe the different members of the community. It stands for "lesbian" (referring to females who are attracted to other females), "gay" (males who are attracted to members of their own sex), "bisexual" (individuals who are attracted to members of both sexes), "transgender" (people who identify as a gender different from the one assigned at birth), and "questioning" (people who are uncertain of their sexual orientation or gender identity). Q may also stand for "queer." In the past, it was used as a homophobic slur. Now, however, many members of the LGBTQ community use it as a blanket label for all nonheterosexual people.

In addition, transgender people, whose gender identity does not define their sexual orientation, often use multiple labels to

Where Do LGBT People Live?

LGBT people live in every state in the United States. This map shows what proportion of each state's population identify as lesbian, gay, bisexual, or transgender. The Williams Institute, a national think tank at the UCLA School of Law, developed this map using the Gallup Daily tracking survey. It interviews and tracks the attitudes and behaviors of one thousand American adults, 350 days a year. Survey respondents were asked: Do you personally identify as lesbian, gay, bisexual, or transgender? Those who self-identify as any of these are included in the data used to create this map.

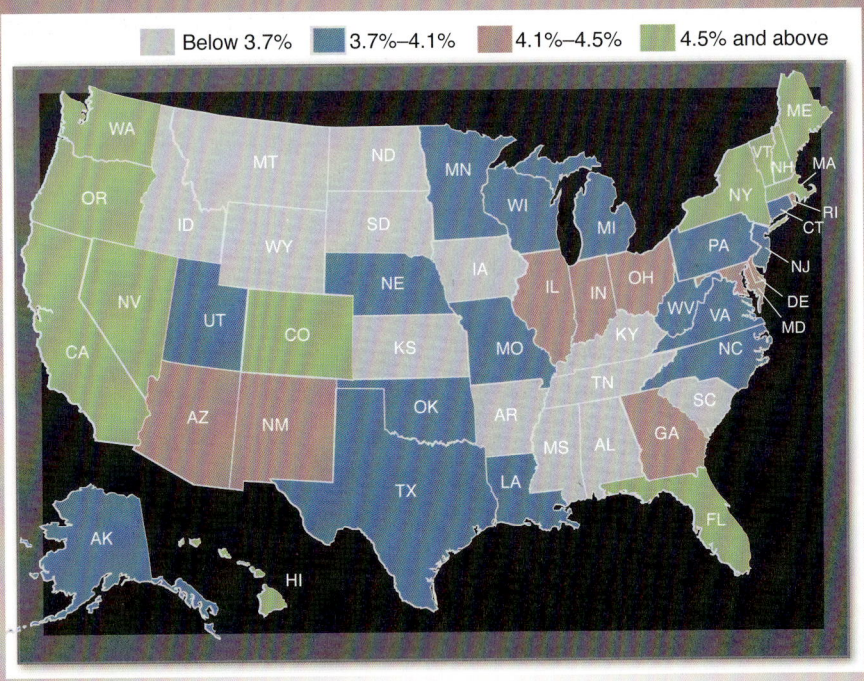

Source: "LGBT Demographic Data Interactive," April 2019. Los Angeles, CA: The Williams Institute, UCLA School of Law. https://williamsinstitute.law.ucla.edu.

describe themselves. It is a widespread misconception that all transgender people are homosexuals. In reality, just like any other person, a transgender individual's sexual orientation may fall anywhere in the sexual spectrum. Cameron, a transgender man, explains: "Gender is one variable in a person's identity and sexual orientation is another variable. The two are not connected. Being trans [is] not the next step to being gay. They are similar in that they are both breaking gender rules. Gay people are breaking rules about who they are supposed to sleep with, and trans people are breaking rules about what gender they are supposed to be."[3]

Many Challenges

Not all Americans accept LGBTQ people. Some have a negative attitude or an irrational fear of LGBTQ individuals. This type of prejudice is known as homophobia (prejudice against homosexuals) or transphobia (prejudice against transgender people). Some of these individuals insult, harass, assault, and discriminate against LGBTQ people. Because there is no federal law that explicitly prohibits discrimination based on a person's sexual orientation or gender identity, LGBTQ individuals have little legal recourse if they are denied services, housing, or employment, among other injustices. They must depend on state laws to protect them. However, the majority of states do not have laws barring discrimination based on a person's sexual orientation or gender identification.

As a nation, the United States has always prided itself on being a just society in which the laws reflect the rights of every citizen, no matter their differences. Yet LGBTQ Americans still face injustice. This should concern everyone. As Petra, a member of the LGBTQ community, says, "All anybody is trying to do is live their lives and be given the service, be treated with respect as anyone else is treated. All we want is equality."[4]

CHAPTER ONE

A Troubling History

In 1982 a gay man named Michael Hardwick was arrested in his Atlanta home for having consensual sex with another man. At the time, a number of states had laws, known as sodomy laws, which criminalized oral and anal sex. Because sodomy laws were rarely used to penalize heterosexual couples, Hardwick challenged the constitutionality of the law. He argued that it unfairly targeted homosexuals. The US Supreme Court disagreed with Hardwick. In 1986, it upheld the constitutionality of the law on the grounds that sex between homosexuals was immoral and states had the constitutional right to criminalize immoral behavior.

Legislating Morality

Sodomy laws were first enacted during colonial times, and were not declared unconstitutional until 2003. Throughout US history there have been a number of laws legislating morality. Many of these criminalized the conduct of LGBTQ people, who, until the later part of the twentieth century, were all labeled *homosexuals*. For instance, at different times in history, laws legislating morality made it illegal to be openly gay, participate in same-gender sexual activity, dance with a same-sex partner, or wear clothes that were not considered gender appropriate.

There are a number of reasons why LGBTQ people have faced bias. Religious doctrine is one of the most significant. Until recently, most religions condemned homosexuality, teaching that same-sex relationships are unnatural and perverse. Most Americans accepted this dogma, and some still do.

Medical science, too, impacted attitudes toward LGBTQ individuals. Until the late twentieth century, homosexuality was considered a mental illness. Many LGBTQ people were institutionalized and administered painful and ineffective treatments, including electric shock therapy, which involved the application of electric shocks to the patient's brain; lobotomies, which are a type of brain surgery; and/or castration in an effort to "cure" them. Facing a medical diagnosis, some LGBTQ individuals voluntarily sought treatment. Others were involuntarily committed to a mental institution by misguided family members or by the criminal justice system. For example, in 1947 in Illinois, anyone convicted of homosexual behavior was sent to a psychiatric prison, where they typically received cruel treatments until they were deemed to be "recovered," at which point they faced up to ten years in prison.

Unrelenting Discrimination

Indeed, homophobia was especially virulent in the twentieth century. After World War I, anti-vice groups formed. They claimed that homosexuals posed a moral threat to society. Many Americans believed them. As a result, the police initiated frequent raids on places where LGBTQ individuals might be found. Suspects were arrested and charged with sodomy, indecent behavior, or disorderly conduct.

The military, too, feared that homosexuals were spreading immorality in their ranks. After World War II, it began investigations to identify and discharge homosexual troops. As part of the process, service members were commanded to testify against each other. According to Pat Bond, who was a member of the Women's Army Corps at the time, "Every day there were court-martials and trials—you were there testifying against your friends, or they

> "Every day there were court-martials and trials—you were there testifying against your friends, or they were testifying against you . . . until you got afraid to look your neighbor in the eye."[5]
>
> —Pat Bond, a lesbian and Women's Army Corps veteran

were testifying against you . . . until you got afraid to look your neighbor in the eye."[5] Indeed, in the 1950s about two thousand suspected gay troops were dishonorably discharged each year and denied benefits.

The Cold War and the threat of communism escalated the hysteria. In the late 1940s and 1950s, lawmakers worried that closeted homosexual government workers were susceptible to blackmail by Communists who might threaten to expose their sexual orientation if they did not hand over classified documents. Therefore, in 1947 President Harry Truman directed the State Department to fire any suspected homosexuals in order to protect national security; a

At different times in history, laws legislating morality made it illegal to be openly gay and participate in same-gender sexual activity. Until recently, most religions condemned homosexuality.

committee was created to identify and root out homosexuals in the government. By 1953 homosexuals had been banned from being employed by any federal agency or private contractor connected to the government. Many state and local governments instituted similar bans, as did a great number of private businesses. Thousands of LGBTQ people lost their jobs and were barred from future employment. It was not until 1973 that a federal court ruled that people could not be fired from a federal job because of their sexual orientation.

Not surprisingly, in an effort to protect themselves, most people kept their sexual orientation and/or gender identity secret. "Everybody was in the closet," recalls gay writer and historian Samuel Steward. "There were no marches, no organizations, nothing like that. We lived under an umbrella of ignorance."[6]

> "Everybody was in the closet. There were no marches, no organizations, nothing like that. We lived under an umbrella of ignorance."[6]
>
> —Samuel Steward, a gay writer and historian

Fighting Back

In the mid-twentieth century, LGBTQ people were not the only minority group in the United States facing prejudice and discrimination. The Civil Rights Act of 1964 was enacted to grant equal rights to oppressed Americans. It made discriminating against people based on race, color, religion, sex, or national original illegal. However, sexual orientation and gender identity are not specifically mentioned as a protected class. The term *sex* as it is used in the Civil Rights Act has traditionally been interpreted as referring to discrimination against women. Because of this, even after the Civil Rights Act was passed, LGBTQ people continued to be harassed and discriminated against. Fearing reprisals, most LGBTQ individuals submissively accepted this treatment.

That changed on June 27, 1969, when the police raided the Stonewall Inn, a bar in New York City that catered to an LGBTQ clientele. At that time, the police routinely raided bars frequented by homosexuals, where they arrested patrons on charges of immorality

Important Terms

A number of terms are used by social scientists when discussing sexual orientation, gender identity, and LGBTQ people. Members of the LGBTQ community also use these terms when describing themselves. The list below defines some of the most commonly used terms:

androgynous: A person whose appearance is not distinguishably masculine or feminine.

bicurious: A person who is curious about having sexual relations with someone of the same gender.

cisgender: A person whose gender identity aligns with the one assigned at birth.

coming out: The process in which a person accepts his or her sexual orientation and gender identity and shares it with others.

gender dysphoria: A medical term used to describe when a person's assigned birth gender is not the same as the one with which he or she identifies.

gender expression: The gender in which people present themselves to others; most people's gender expression matches up with the gender assigned at birth.

gender fluid or nonbinary: A person who does not exclusively identify with a single gender, who may feel more like a male on some days and more like a female on others.

intersex: A term used to describe a person born with both male and female genitals.

pansexual: A person who is attracted to people of any gender or gender identity.

queer: A term, which was once derogatory, that is now used in a positive way by LGBTQ people to describe themselves.

without any resistance. In fact, New York's police inspector at the time, Seymour Pine, said homosexuals were "easy arrests. They never gave you trouble. Everybody behaved."[7]

Only this time, the LGBTQ community did not behave. Frustrated by years of unfair treatment, the bar patrons resisted. They threw beer bottles, garbage, coins, and bricks at the stunned police officers. As word of the uprising spread, the street filled with angry LGBTQ people shouting, "Gay Power." They overturned cars, broke windows, and physically attacked the police officers. As Sylvia Rivera, a transgender woman, recalls, "I wanted to do every destructive thing that I could think of at that time to hurt anyone that had hurt us through the years."[8]

Riot police, swinging nightsticks and spraying tear gas, were called in. But the crowd refused to be cowed. The rioting lasted until about four in the morning and then broke out again the next two nights. According to Rivera, "A lot of heads were bashed. . . . A lot of people were hurt. But it didn't hurt their true feelings. They all came back for more and more. Nothing . . . could stop us at that time or at any time in the future."[9]

The Stonewall Inn bar (pictured) located in New York City has catered to LGBTQ clientele since the 1960s. The Stonewall uprising of 1969 is often credited with being the start of the gay pride movement.

Indeed, the Stonewall uprising is often credited with being the start of the gay pride movement. According to historian Lillian Faderman, it "was the shot heard round the world . . . crucial because it sounded the rally for the movement, it became an emblem for gay and lesbian power."[10]

Inspired by the events at the Stonewall Inn, more and more LGBTQ individuals came out of the closet. Gay rights groups began to pop up all over the country. They organized protest marches and demonstrations, lobbied politicians, and spoke to the media. In fact, a year after the Stonewall rebellion, they organized the first gay pride parade in New York City. An estimated five thousand to twenty thousand people participated. Never before had the public seen so many proud LGBTQ people in one place.

One Step Forward, Two Steps Back

A lot of things changed for LGBTQ people in the next few decades as a consequence of these efforts. Some of these changes were positive, bringing them greater rights and acceptance, but other changes aimed to keep them down. Among the positive changes was the passage of a number of city and state ordinances protecting LGBTQ people from discrimination and supporting gay rights. For example, Oregon and Colorado repealed their sodomy laws in 1971; and Hawaii and California made homosexuality legal in 1972 and 1975, respectively. People in those states could now be open about their sexual orientation without fear of arrest. Cities also took action. In 1972 East Lansing and Ann Arbor, both in Michigan, and San Francisco, California, became the first cities to pass homosexual rights ordinances. And in 1977 Harvey Milk, an openly gay man, was elected to serve on San Francisco's Board of Supervisors. Yet that victory was short-lived. Milk and George Moscone, the city's pro-LGBTQ mayor, were assassinated a year later by a homophobe.

Many Americans felt threatened by the progress the LGBTQ community was making. Anita Bryant, a popular singer and religious fundamentalist, was one of the most vocal. In 1977, after

Dade County, Florida, passed an ordinance that prohibited discrimination against homosexuals, she organized a campaign to repeal the ordinance and keep other cities from enacting similar policies. Using the media and her celebrity status, Bryant falsely claimed that gay men were child molesters who lured young boys into their ranks. "As a mother," she proclaimed, "I know homosexuals cannot biologically reproduce children; therefore, they must recruit our children."[11] Bryant's campaign successfully overturned the Dade County ordinance, as well as similar ordinances in Minnesota, Oregon, and Kansas.

Multiple groups opposed to granting LGBTQ people equal rights repeated the allegation. In an effort to counter these falsehoods, in 1979 more than one hundred thousand LGBTQ protesters and their supporters marched on Washington demanding equal rights. The LGBTQ community hoped that this peaceful demonstration would show the American public that LGBTQ people were not dangerous, thereby garnering support for their cause.

> "As a mother, I know homosexuals cannot biologically reproduce children; therefore, they must recruit our children."[11]
>
> —Anita Bryant, a singer and anti-LGBTQ rights activist

However, the human immunodeficiency virus (HIV) and acquired immunodeficiency syndrome (AIDS) epidemic, which began in 1981 and at first mainly impacted gay men, thwarted this plan. According to a report by the British Academy, an organization that studies people, culture, and society throughout the world, by 1995 one out of every nine gay men in the United States had been diagnosed with the disease. Worse still, one out of every fifteen had died from it. Yet many Americans were unsympathetic. A 1992 survey conducted by the Public Religion Research Institute found that 36 percent of Americans believed that AIDS was God's way of punishing homosexuals for immoral behavior. And, even though the disease cannot be spread through casual contact, many Americans were terrified that they would contract it. They feared that even the slightest contact with an LGBTQ person would infect them.

LGBTQ people became pariahs. Some were fired from their jobs, evicted from their homes, and brutally attacked on the streets. Politicians considered quarantining all LGBTQ people, but they did little else to stop the epidemic. Gay rights groups pressured the government to fund research to fight the disease. Largely due to their efforts, a treatment that makes AIDS a manageable disease became available in 1996, causing AIDS deaths to drop by about 50 percent in that year alone.

Broken Promises

Despite these setbacks, the LGBTQ community continued to lobby for equal rights. The election of President Bill Clinton in 1992 raised their hopes. During his election campaign, he vowed to end the ban on homosexual men and women in the military. However, when he tried to keep his promise, he was met with strong opposition from anti-LGBTQ groups. Yet he refused to give up entirely. In 1993 he came up with a compromise known as Don't Ask, Don't Tell, which allowed homosexual troops to serve in the military as long as they kept their sexual orientation hidden. LGBTQ activists were not happy with the compromise. They insisted it forced LGBTQ troops to hide who they were in order to serve their country, thus sending a message that discriminating against LGBTQ people was acceptable. Don't Ask, Don't Tell was repealed in 2010. During the time it was in effect, more than fourteen thousand homosexual troops were dishonorably discharged, often not because they were indiscreet but because someone told on them.

While Clinton was wrangling with the military ban on homosexuals, some LGBTQ couples were challenging various state bans on same-sex marriage, which they charged violated their civil rights. Fearing these challenges would cause some states to recognize same-sex marriage, in 1996 the US Congress passed the Defense of Marriage Act. It defined marriage as a union between one man and one woman, and it allowed states to refuse to recognize same-sex marriages granted under the laws of another state. Under political pressure, Clinton signed the act into law.

The election of President Bill Clinton (pictured) in 1992 raised the hopes of the LGBTQ community. During his election campaign, he vowed to end the ban on homosexual men and women in the military.

Significant Advances in the Twenty-First Century

By the start of the new millennium, more and more LGBTQ people were unashamedly disclosing their sexual orientation and gender identity, including many popular celebrities. As the public became more familiar with LGBTQ individuals, some became more willing to grant them equal rights, but others counterattacked. For instance, Massachusetts became the first state to legalize same-sex marriage in 2004. But that same year, thirteen other states passed state constitutional amendments defining marriage as a union between a man and a woman. Still, acceptance of same-sex marriage was gradually increasing. By 2012 it was legal in nine states. And, in 2013 the US Supreme Court overturned the Defense of Marriage Act. A year later, thirty-seven states had legalized same-sex marriage. Then, on June 26, 2015, the Supreme Court gave same-sex couples the constitutional right to marry nationwide.

Life Before the Stonewall Uprising

In an interview with broadcast journalist Amy Goodman, members of the LGBTQ community recall what their lives were like in the mid-twentieth century:

> "My name is Randy Wicker. I was the first openly gay person to appear on radio in 1962 and on television in 1964. . . . In the era before Stonewall, people felt a need to hide because of the precarious legal position they were in. They would lose their jobs. There was a great hostility, socially speaking, in the sense if people found out you were gay they assumed you were a communist or a child molester or any of another dozen stereotypes that were rampant in the public media at the time.
>
> I'm Jheri Faire. . . . I started a gay lifestyle in 1948. . . . At that time, if there was even a suspicion that you were a lesbian, you were fired from your job, and you were in such a position of disgrace that you slunk out without saying goodbye even to the people that liked you and you liked, never even bothered to clean your desk. You just disappeared. . . .
>
> My name is Sylvia Rivera. My name before that was Ray Rivera, until I started dressing in drag in 1961. The era before Stonewall was a hard era. There was always the gay bashings on the drag queens [men dressing as women] by heterosexual men, women and the police.

Quoted in *Democracy Now!*, "Stonewall Riots 40th Anniversary: A Look Back at the Uprising That Launched the Modern Gay Rights Movement," June 26, 2009. www.democracynow.org.

Having the right to marry not only allowed same-sex couples to openly affirm and celebrate their love, but it also gave them the same legal and financial rights, protections, and benefits that opposite-sex married couples have. These include spousal health insurance and Social Security benefits, the right to make health care and end-of-life decisions for each other, and tax and inheritance benefits, among other things. As Shirley Winslow, a lesbian who married her longtime partner in 2015, explains, "For us it's a symbol of our relationship. We want to show everyone else out there who may disapprove of same-sex marriage that we are no different than anyone else. After 25 years of being together and being denied the basic civil rights of married couples, it was time to take a stand and stand up for ourselves and get the recognition that we deserve."[12]

The support of President Barack Obama also helped LGBTQ people. Among his many contributions, in 2010 his administration struck down Don't Ask, Don't Tell, making it legal for openly gay and lesbian troops to serve in the military without reprisal. Obama also changed military policy that banned transgender people from the military; in 2017, however, President Donald Trump attempted to reinstate that ban.

> "After 25 years of being together and being denied the basic civil rights of married couples, it was time to take a stand and stand up for ourselves and get the recognition that we deserve."[12]
>
> —Shirley Winslow, a spouse in a same-sex marriage

Clearly, LGBTQ people have come a long way, but they still have a ways to go before they achieve total equality and complete acceptance. As actress and LGBTQ rights supporter Lynda Carter says, "The fight will still have to go on—it will never be over, and we've always got to work hard . . . but I think that the larger tides really are changing."[13]

CHAPTER TWO

Growing Up LGBTQ Is Not Easy

Many LGBTQ people have experienced prejudice at some point in their lives. LGBTQ children, adolescents, and young adults, in particular, are often subjected to bullying, insults, harassment, and discrimination. This hurtful treatment can take place in many settings, including at school, at home, and at houses of worship. Wherever such treatment occurs, it marks LGBTQ youth as different by attacking their dignity and marginalizing them. As a result, it impacts how they view themselves and how they interact with others. For instance, it is not unusual for LGBTQ young people to grow up hearing and believing insensitive and derogatory comments and mistruths about homosexual and transgender people, which makes them feel ashamed of who they are. As Stewart Taylor, a gay singer and songwriter, explains, "Much of our society is still extremely homophobic. And many kids get the message that being gay is the worst thing they can be."[14]

Problems in School

Many LGBTQ students find themselves the target of verbal abuse by their classmates. Children and adolescents are often uncomfortable with anyone who is out of the ordinary, and they can be cruel to those whom they perceive to be different. Plus, some young people are influenced by the opinions of homophobic and transphobic adults whom they admire. Others are hostile because they are insecure about their own sexuality. According to PFLAG, an organization that supports LGBTQ individuals and their parents, nine out of ten LGBTQ youths experience some form of harassment at school. Laurel Slongwhite, a medical doctor and a member of the LGBTQ community, was frequently mocked by her classmates. She remembers, "I was actually afraid to go to school because I got made fun of all the time. And once I got there, on any given day, I was afraid to move. Because if I moved, they'd see me, they'd notice me. And every time somebody noticed me, they would make fun of me. They said terrible things."[15]

> "Much of our society is still extremely homophobic. And many kids get the message that being gay is the worst thing they can be."[14]
>
> —Stewart Taylor, a gay singer and songwriter

Insults are directed at LGBTQ youths who are open about their sexual orientation and gender identity as well as those who have not yet come to terms with their own sexuality but are perceived to be LGBTQ by their peers. While you cannot tell if someone is LGBTQ by the way they look, some young people have mannerisms, pursue hobbies, or wear clothes not associated with their gender, or they show no romantic attraction to members of the opposite sex—all of which makes them stand out and identifies them as different. Jenn Wagner-Martin, a mental health counselor, remembers that even though she had not come to terms with her sexual identity, some of her classmates had labeled her as gay. "They'd leave notes on my locker or shout out 'lezzy' and 'dyke' when I was walking down the hall. This would happen every day. It was tough. It was especially hard to endure because you have to go to school every day."[16]

Often, the harassment does not end with mockery and insults. LGBTQ students report being intimidated, bullied, and assaulted. A 2017 survey of more than twelve thousand LGBTQ

Many LGBTQ students find themselves the target of verbal abuse by their classmates. Adolescents can be cruel to those whom they perceive to be different.

teens, conducted jointly by the Human Rights Campaign Foundation and the University of Connecticut, found that 73 percent of survey respondents experienced verbal threats at school, 30 percent experienced physical threats, and 70 percent experienced bullying because of their LGBTQ identity or perceived identity. As video game and film director Khris Brown recalls,

> People said horrible things to me every day, they even made death threats. Kids would throw garbage at me, open my locker and slice open all my pictures, tear apart my books and throw them all over the locker room, pour soda on my stuff, throw my clothes all over the gym locker room. This kind of stuff happened every day in junior and senior high school. And let me tell you it got a little wearing.[17]

Because of being treated unjustly, some LGBTQ students become isolated. They avoid participating in extracurricular activities or attending school events. It is not unusual for them to miss classes in order to avoid daily abuse. In fact, according to a report by GLSEN, an organization that works to make schools safe for LGBTQ students, LGBTQ students are twice as likely as non-LGBTQ students to have skipped school due to feeling unsafe or uncomfortable there. "Thinking back to high school," admits Salem Whit, a transgender individual, "I don't know how my grades were good enough to graduate. . . . I skipped classes . . . I quit every extracurricular. I stopped participating in sports, gym, drama. . . . I even stopped talking for a while."[18]

Varying Policies

Faced with these issues, many schools have instituted policies that support and protect LGBTQ students. These schools have clubs, such as the Gay Straight Alliance, that bring straight and LGBTQ students together. They include LGBTQ history and issues in their curriculum, and they have books that feature LGBTQ characters in the school media center. Teachers often display "safe space" stickers in their classrooms, which let students know that everyone, no matter their sexual orientation or gender identity, is welcomed and accepted. "Those little signs are great," says Delaware teen Queen Cornish, "because they let you know that the teacher is going to respect your identity."[19]

But not all schools have these policies. There is no federal law that protects students from bullying, harassment, or discrimination in school because of sexual orientation or gender identity. It is up to states, local school districts, or school administrators to set such policies. Therefore, in some schools, LGBTQ students are not treated the same as other students. In these schools, LGBTQ young people often refrain from reporting bullying and harassment because their complaints are typically ignored or discounted. According to the GLSEN report, 53.3 percent of LGBTQ students say that they have not reported bullying because they doubt there

Hurtful Words

LGBTQ youths frequently experience insensitive verbal slurs. These insults are often deliberate. However, sometimes they are unintentional. In these cases, the speaker does not mean to offend LGBTQ individuals but does so out of ignorance, confusion, or insensitivity. This sometimes occurs when others do not use a transgender individual's preferred pronouns or name. Even if this is done out of ignorance or confusion, it still disrespects transgender youth. Using the pronouns and name that a person goes by is a way of respecting that person's gender identity. Not doing so makes transgender individuals feel that their gender identity is unimportant to the speaker, or that the speaker does not accept who they are.

In other incidences, offensive comments are made in jest. For example, many young people use the slang phrase "that's so gay" to indicate that something is ridiculous, bad, or stupid. Even though the speaker may not mean to offend gay people, in general, or any one gay person, in particular, using terms associated with the LGBTQ community in a negative manner degrades LGBTQ people. When someone says something bad or ridiculous is "gay," they are essentially saying that being gay is bad or ridiculous.

would be an appropriate response. Of those who did report it, 60.3 percent said school staff did nothing in response or advised the student to ignore the problem. This lack of response occurs for a variety of reasons. In some cases, school personnel may be sympathetic to LGBTQ students but do not have the knowledge or training to deal with the issues they face. In other cases, homophobia plays a role. For instance, a high school freshman explained that when she reported being bullied because of her sexual orientation, a homophobic school administrator told her, "We can't help you because you chose to be this."[20]

Adding to the problem, policies in some schools prohibit clubs that support the LGBTQ community, ban books with LGBTQ characters, prohibit classroom assignments or discussions that relate to LGBTQ issues (even in health classes), and discourage same-sex couples from attending school events. In these schools, it is not unusual for students to be removed from class or sent home for dressing in clothes that are not considered gender appropriate. In one incident, for example, a cafeteria worker in an Ohio high school denied a male student lunch because he was wearing a bow in his hair.

Plus, many schools and school districts deny transgender students access to gender-neutral bathrooms and changing rooms. This policy not only embarrasses transgender teens but also threatens their safety. A survey of 3,673 transgender middle and high school students, reported in 2019 in the

School personnel may be sympathetic to LGBTQ students but often do not have the knowledge or training to deal with the issues the students might face.

medical journal *Pediatrics*, found that 35 percent of respondents who were forced to use gendered facilities had been sexually assaulted. As Emme, a transgender teen, explains,

> Most trans youth have real everyday obstacles that impact their mental health, social capacity, and ease of movement. Bathrooms, changing rooms, and otherwise gendered . . . facilities are some of the most intimidating places. Some trans youth plan their entire day around avoiding school bathrooms and changing. For so many of us, our daily movements are dictated by fear.[21]

Insensitivity, Shame, Guilt, and Sin

School is not the only place where LGBTQ young people are disrespected. In church, a large number of LGBTQ youths are exposed to religious dogma that shames, insults, and frightens them. Although many religious denominations affirm and welcome LGBTQ people, others consider homosexuality a grave sin and openly condemn LGBTQ people. Hearing homophobic and transphobic messages in their houses of worship causes some young LGBTQ worshippers to question their self-worth. "I was in church every week hearing the pastor preach that gays are going to hell. . . . I dealt with a lot of inner turmoil and self-hatred for a very long time,"[22] confesses gay journalist and human rights activist Dwayne Steward.

Homophobic and transphobic doctrine also affects the way other people treat LGBTQ young people. Those who accept these teachings tend to be openly hostile toward LGBTQ individuals. As a result, some young people try to hide their sexual orientation and gender identity from members of their religious community and try to present themselves as heterosexuals. They fear that

> "Some trans youth plan their entire day around avoiding school bathrooms and changing. For so many of us, our daily movements are dictated by fear."[21]
>
> —Emme, a transgender teen

LGBTQ Youth and Cyberbullying

LGBTQ youth are often the target of cyberbullying and harassment. According to GLSEN, an organization that works to prevent the bullying of LGBTQ students, 42 percent of LGBTQ young people ages eleven to twenty-two have experienced cyberbullying. This figure is about three times greater than that for non-LGBTQ youth.

LGBTQ young people report being threatened, sexually harassed, and insulted online. They also report receiving offensive texts from their peers and having embarrassing photos and personal or false information being spread about them on social media. Because of something they said in a private chat or text, some young people have had their sexual orientation or gender identity revealed online without their consent.

GLSEN reports that many LGBTQ youths rely on the internet to get information about being LGBTQ. They are five times more likely to search for information on sexuality, almost twice as likely to search for health and medical information, and four times more likely to search for information on HIV/AIDS than non-LGBTQ young people. Some LGBTQ youth also use the internet to connect with and get support from other LGBTQ individuals and groups. Because of this, many young people are reluctant to report cyberbullying incidents to their parents. They fear that, in an effort to protect them, their parents might restrict their online access.

if they were to expose their true selves, they would be rejected. Says Ely Winkler, an LGBTQ activist and social worker who hid his sexual orientation from his Orthodox Jewish community, "It's hard to be proud of who you are when your community tells you not to be. When you feel that no one around you will accept you."[23]

Prejudice at Home

In many cases, immediate and extended family members accept and support LGBTQ young people, but some youths encounter bigotry at home. Bigotry can lead people to make judgmental

> "It's hard to be proud of who you are when your community tells you not to be. When you feel that no one around you will accept you."[23]
>
> —Ely Winkler, an LGBTQ activist and social worker

statements and insensitive jokes. Being exposed to this can make young people feel rejected by their loved ones. Erika Wagner-Martin, a Wisconsin mental health counselor, faced this type of situation as an adolescent. She recalls, "While my immediate family wasn't particularly anti-gay or homophobic, in any ways, certain members of my extended family were. Many times at Thanksgiving or Christmas or Easter I would have to endure anti-gay comments, and I just knew that it wasn't going to be okay with some of my family to be who I was. And that was really hard."[24]

Indeed, in some families, when young people reveal their sexual orientation or gender identity, they are made to feel that there is something wrong with them. Some misguided parents have LGBTQ kids undergo conversion therapy. This therapy, which is typically administered by counselors or religious advisers, can be emotionally abusive. It is based on the erroneous theory that being homosexual or transgender is a choice. Therefore, with proper guidance, LGBTQ young people can and will chose to change their sexual orientation and gender identity. Practitioners try to achieve this goal by persuading individuals that their thoughts and feelings are wicked and abnormal. According to a young man who was subjected to conversion therapy when he was fifteen years old, "Their goal was to get us to hate ourselves for being LGBTQ."[25]

There is no evidence that a person's sexual orientation or gender identity can be changed, or that conversion therapy works. In fact, it appears to do more harm than good, causing some individuals to develop depression, low self-esteem, and suicidal thoughts. Many medical organizations, including the American Medical Association and the American Psychiatric Association, have condemned it. And, as of 2019, nineteen states have banned it for minors due to the damage it inflicts on young people. Yet the practice persists in many states.

Becoming Homeless

In other cases, parents reject and abandon LGBTQ teens when they reveal their sexual orientation or gender identity. If these young people do not have friends or other loved ones with whom they can stay, they often become homeless. That is exactly what happened to one LGBTQ teen. He says, "My father didn't respect me for who I am because he don't like bisexual people or gay people so [when] . . . I came out to him . . . he just kicked me out, because he couldn't take it."[26]

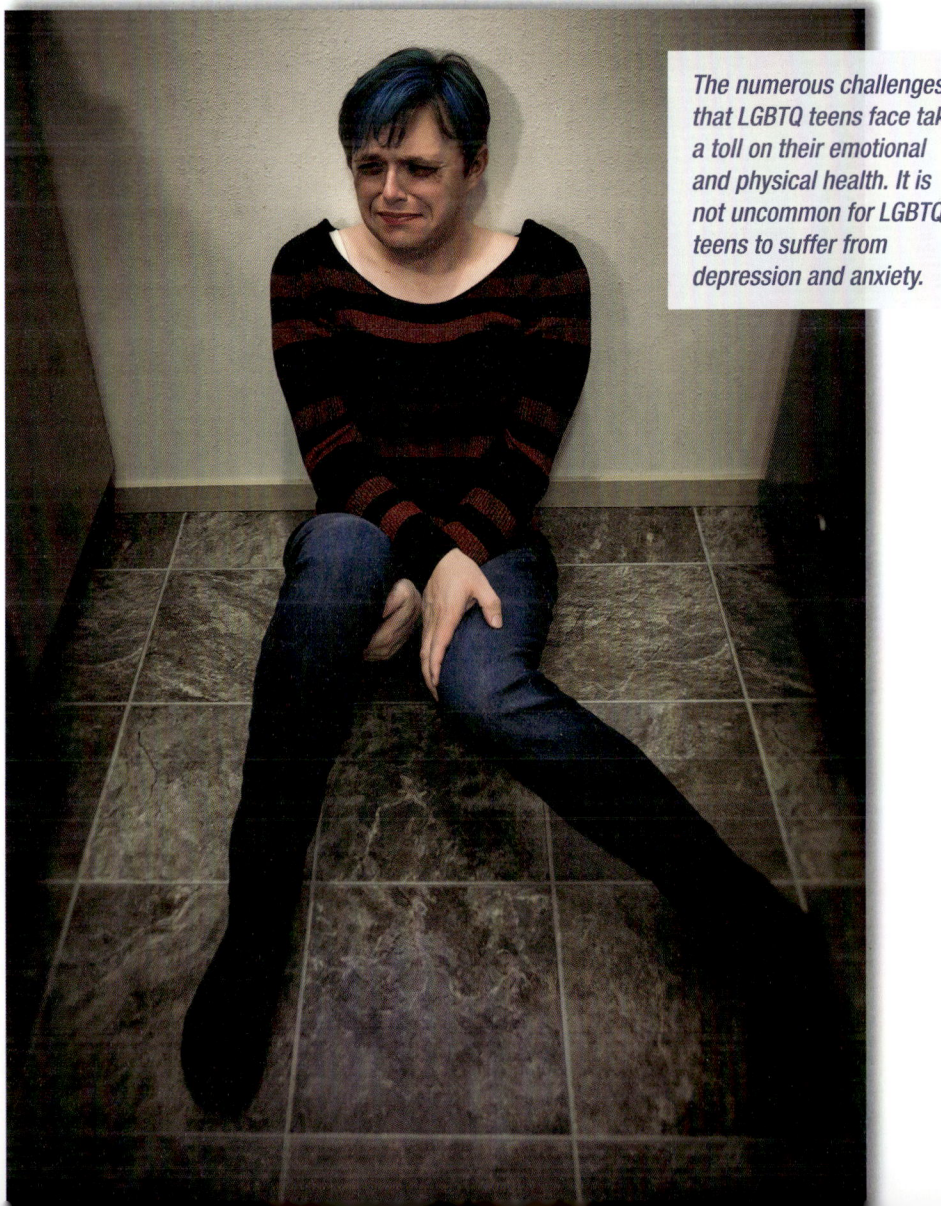

The numerous challenges that LGBTQ teens face take a toll on their emotional and physical health. It is not uncommon for LGBTQ teens to suffer from depression and anxiety.

According to True Colors, an organization that works to end homelessness among LGBTQ youths, 25 percent of LGBTQ teens are thrown out of their homes at some point after coming out to their parents. Moreover, some LGBTQ young people leave home voluntarily because their parents make them feel unwelcome. True Colors reports that of the 1.6 million young Americans who experience homelessness each year, 40 percent identify as LGBTQ. Since LGBTQ young people make up about 10 percent of the total youth population in the United States, this figure is quite high.

Being homeless is dangerous. It is especially so for LGBTQ young people. The National Coalition for the Homeless reports that homeless LGBTQ youth are more than seven times more likely to experience sexual violence than other homeless young people. Compounding the problem, it is difficult for homeless LGBTQ teens to find homeless shelters that accept and respect them. In fact, some homeless shelters turn away transgender people.

Dangerous Consequences

The numerous challenges that LGBTQ youths face take a toll on their emotional and physical health. It is not uncommon for LGBTQ young people to suffer from depression, anxiety, loneliness, low self-esteem, insomnia, headaches, and digestive problems. Some young people turn to drugs and alcohol in an attempt to self-medicate. The National Human Rights Campaign, an organization dedicated to supporting LGBTQ people, reports that LGBTQ teens are twice as likely as other teens to abuse drugs and alcohol.

Some young people feel so hopeless that they consider ending their lives. Research published in *Pediatrics* indicates that LGBTQ youth are three times as likely to consider suicide and are twice as likely to attempt it as non-LGBTQ young people. A 2019 survey of more than thirty-four thousand LGBTQ youth conducted by the Trevor Project, an organization that provides suicide prevention services for LGBTQ youth, found that 39 percent of all respondents seriously considered attempting suicide in the past year. As author David E. Newton explains, "For a number of gay, lesbian, bisexual, and transgender youth, the very thought of having to survive on a day-to-day basis in the face of verbal and physical harassment from so many different people . . . is more than one can take. The only remaining option may seem to be to commit suicide."[27]

Of course, suicide is never a good option. And growing up is not easy for anyone. It is especially difficult for LGBTQ youth who face unique challenges. Yet despite the issues and challenges they face, most LGBTQ youth go on to live happy and productive lives.

CHAPTER THREE

The Long Reach of Discrimination

Young people are not the only members of the LGBTQ community who are treated unfairly. LGBTQ individuals frequently face discrimination in multiple areas of their lives. Since there is no federal law that explicitly protects people from discrimination based on sexual orientation or gender identity, in many states LGBTQ people are treated by a different standard.

Discrimination in the Workplace

Some LGBTQ individuals face discrimination in the workplace. Although many companies have nondiscrimination policies that include sexual orientation and gender identity, some do not. Twenty-one percent of LGBTQ respondents to multiple surveys conducted by the Williams Institute, a think tank at the University of California, Los Angeles, School of Law, reported being discriminated against in hiring, promotions, and pay. Respondents recounted being turned down for jobs they were qualified for and not being promoted or paid at the same rate as their peers.

LGBTQ individuals also reported being suspended, fired, or forced to resign from a position because of their sexual orientation or gender identity. Take the case of a Texas art teacher named Stacy Bailey. In 2017 school administrators ordered the award-winning teacher to resign after she displayed a photo of her same-sex fiancée in a place where her students could see it. School administrators claimed that because same-sex marriage is politically controversial, by sharing the photo with her students, Bailey was making a political statement. This violated the school district's policy prohibiting teachers from airing their personal political views in the classroom. Bailey insisted her actions were not political in nature. She maintained that she was targeted because she was open about her sexual orientation. "What happened to me is most gay teachers' worst nightmare," she said. "Why aren't straight teachers afraid to talk about their families? Why do they feel comfortable to have a picture of their family on their desk without questioning their safety?"[28]

Bailey sued the school district for discrimination and won the case in February 2020. A number of similar cases are working their way through the courts. In October 2019 the US Supreme Court heard three cases concerning whether laws prohibiting employment discrimination apply to LGBTQ people. The justices were split in their opinion. A decision on these cases was expected by mid-2020.

> "Why aren't straight teachers afraid to talk about their families? Why do they feel comfortable to have a picture of their family on their desk without questioning their safety?"[28]
>
> —Stacy Bailey, a teacher and lesbian

Harassment at Work

Even if LGBTQ individuals do not face outright discrimination in the workplace, some report being harassed and bullied by homophobic and transphobic coworkers. A 2018 survey by CareerBuilder, an employment website, found that 56 percent of LGBTQ respondents reported being repeatedly bullied on the job. They described being mocked, intimidated, and humiliated by coworkers who, among other things, falsely accused them of making mistakes, ignored their comments and recommendations, criticized and gossiped about them, and excluded them from projects, meetings, and social functions.

In an effort to avoid both harassment and discrimination in the workplace, many LGBTQ workers hide their sexual orientation and gender identity from their employers and coworkers. In a 2017 survey conducted by National Public Radio (NPR), 46 percent of LGBTQ respondents said that they were closeted at work. These individuals carefully guard what they say and do in order to conceal details about their lives. They avoid displaying family photos, talking about a same-sex spouse or partner, or bringing their partner to company events. Some change their mannerisms, speech, and the way they dress in order to appear heterosexual. As David, a gay man, explains, "I'm trying to minimize the bias against me by changing my presentation in the corporate world. I lower my voice in meetings to make it sound less feminine and avoid wearing anything but a black suit."[29]

In multiple surveys, a significant percentage of LGBTQ respondents reported being discriminated against in hiring. They recounted being turned down for jobs they were qualified for.

Hiding one's identity is stressful. Those who do so live with the ongoing fear that they will be discovered. "It makes you totally paranoid about being honest with anyone," says Nita, a lesbian and former educator. "You have to be so careful about what you say, what you do, even how you dress. If you make the slightest slip, you worry that they'll use it against you—find some way to not like you."[30] Not surprisingly, being under this kind of persistent stress can negatively affect a person's emotional and physical health as well as their job performance.

Housing

Housing is another area in which some LGBTQ people face discrimination. The Federal Fair Housing Act does not explicitly protect people from housing discrimination based on sexual orientation or gender identification. And state laws vary widely. LGBTQ people residing in states that do not have antidiscrimination laws based on sexual orientation or gender identity can be refused housing, charged higher-than-normal rents, and evicted from their homes. In the NPR survey, 22 percent of respondents stated they had experienced discrimination when trying to rent an apartment or buy a house. Bias in housing hurts LGBTQ people in many ways. According to Diane K. Levy, a researcher at the Urban Institute, "Differential treatment matters. When people are discriminated against in their housing searches, not only does it go against our collective value of equal opportunity, but it limits their options for where to live, which can affect how they get to work, the schools their children attend, and other facets of their daily lives."[31]

> "When people are discriminated against in their housing searches, . . . it limits their options for where to live, which can affect how they get to work, the schools their children attend, and other facets of their daily lives."[31]
>
> —Diane K. Levy, a researcher at the Urban Institute

Older LGBTQ individuals, in particular, often face housing discrimination when they try to move into senior living facilities. In a study by the Equal Rights Center, older individuals posing as

Discrimination in College Housing

Kaj Baker is a lesbian who was a freshman at the University of Texas at Austin in 2018. Although she had not broken any rules, she was banned from having any guests visit her in her off-campus, privately owned, all-women dormitory. The dormitory houses three hundred college women, but Baker was the only resident prohibited from having guests. When she questioned the dormitory administrator about why she was singled out when she had not broken any rules, Baker was told that in her case, the rules did not matter. The problem, it seemed, was her sexual orientation. The administrator told Baker that other residents had complained because Baker's girlfriend often visited her, and the two frequently studied together in the residence's common lounge area, which made some residents feel uncomfortable. According to Baker, "The list of complaints weren't us doing anything wrong. We weren't harming anyone. We weren't doing PDA [public displays of affection]. We weren't breaking any rules. It was us existing. They told me that girls need to feel safe here, and I asked her if we made people feel unsafe. She said, 'I'm not going there. I'm not going there just yet.'"

Baker released a voice recording of the meeting to the media, alleging discrimination. Although a number of dorm residents have been supportive of her, others have sent her hostile messages online. As a result, Baker moved to another residence.

Quoted in Theresa Braine, "Gay Texas College Student Alleges Discrimination After Dorm Forbids Her to Have Guests," *New York Daily News*, November 29, 2018. www.nydailynews.com.

same-sex and heterosexual couples applied for the same senior housing. In almost half the tests, the same-sex couples were offered fewer housing options and charged higher fees and rents than the heterosexual couples. Ironically, in order to gain residency in some facilities, older LGBTQ people, many of whom have been involved in the fight for LGBTQ rights for decades, have to hide their sexual identities. In an effort to solve this problem, some cities have established LGBTQ-friendly senior living facilities. However, there are usually more applicants than there are units available.

Transgender individuals, too, are also frequent targets of housing discrimination. According to the National Center for Transgender Equality, more than one in ten transgender individuals have been evicted from their homes because of their gender identity. Queen, a transgender woman in North Carolina, was one of this group. She was evicted from her apartment after her landlord learned she was transgender. She was told that the building had been sold and she had to move out immediately, which was untrue. Queen was forced out of her home because of her gender identity.

Bias against LGBTQ people related to housing also comes in more subtle forms. Some members of the LGBTQ community are made to feel unwelcome and unsafe by prejudiced neighbors. Some have consid-

> Housing is an area in which some LGBTQ people face discrimination. In one survey, 22 percent of respondents stated they had experienced discrimination when trying to rent an apartment or buy a house.

ered moving because of the hostility they face. This is especially common in smaller, less diverse communities. Tommy Starling, a gay man who lives in a conservative region of South Carolina with his husband and their two children, has experienced this type of prejudice firsthand: "Somebody said that our kids should be taken away from us and we should be hanged. If it wasn't for my husband's job, we wouldn't be here."[32]

Unequal Health Care

Health care is another area in which some LGBTQ individuals are treated by a different standard. The American Medical Association's code of ethics prohibits physicians from refusing to treat people based on their sexual orientation or gender identity. Yet some health care professionals do just that. According to the Center for American Progress, one in three transgender people has been denied access to medical care because of gender identity. As Kelli Farrow, a transgender woman in Florida, explains,

> Finding doctors that will even treat you is difficult. I can call several providers . . . and I tell the nursing staff or front desk I'm transgender and just want to make sure they see people such as myself, and they come back after speaking with the provider and tell me they don't specialize in people like me, or they don't treat people like me or some other version, and all I'm trying to do is seek a primary care doctor.[33]

Others provide inadequate care or have a hostile or disrespectful attitude toward LGBTQ patients, particularly transgender and HIV-positive patients. According to Dr. Alexis Chavez, a psychiatrist at University of Colorado Health and one of the founders of Colorado's first LGBTQ health clinics,

> LGBTQ patients with HIV that I've seen have told me that sometimes healthcare providers don't really want to touch

them as much, or the provider used some excessive precautions even though it's well-treated, well-controlled HIV where the rates of transmission are very low. . . . I would say that there's certainly still discrimination, and on a number of different levels.[34]

Moreover, many health care professionals have little training in how to treat the special health issues of people receiving cross-sex hormone therapy. This is a treatment that helps transgender people align secondary sexual characteristics, like the development of facial hair or the growth of breasts, with their gender identity. As a result, physicians may provide transgender patients with ineffective or inadequate treatment.

Because of these problems, health clinics that specialize in treating the LGBTQ community have opened in some large cities. But people living in rural areas usually do not have access to these facilities. According to the NPR survey, 41 percent of rural respondents said they would have to travel at least 100 miles (160 km) to receive care in one of these facilities. Indeed, because of discrimination, humiliation, and inadequate treatment, some LGBTQ individuals do not seek care. Yet this is dangerous; not seeking preventive care, for example, puts people at higher risk for undiagnosed heart disease, high blood pressure, and cancer.

Bias in the Criminal Justice System

LGBTQ people, and especially transgender individuals and LGBTQ people of color, are often victimized by the criminal justice system. In some instances, biased police officers target places where LGBTQ people assemble and then charge them with minor infractions like curfew violations or public indecency. In other cases, young homeless members of the LGBTQ community have been arrested for sleeping on the street.

Many LGBTQ individuals, and particularly LGBTQ youth of color, complain of being targeted and harassed by police officers.

A bisexual Latino teen explains that he and his LGBTQ friends have been harassed by law enforcement on multiple occasions:

> The [police] car would just come by and they'd be like, "freeze," and we weren't doing anything, we were just standing across the street from the school. And they would like throw my [skate] board to the side to make sure I didn't like hit them or anything. And then they would just pat me down all types of stuff. One time it was like really crazy. A guy like grabbed my penis and it was just like I don't know. I feel like it got worse, you're stopped and frisked . . . it just got worse.[35]

Indeed, although members of the LGBTQ community are no more likely to commit a crime than anyone else, they are more likely to be charged with a crime than other people and are more likely to be incarcerated. A report by the Center for American Progress and

Two transgender friends take a walk. Nearly 50 percent of all black transgender individuals have been incarcerated at some time in their lives. In comparison, only 5 percent of the total US population has ever been incarcerated.

Discrimination in the Courtroom

Personal prejudices may influence the decisions of jurors in cases involving LGBTQ people. In 1992 Charles Rhines, a gay man, was convicted of stabbing a man to death during a botched robbery. He was sentenced to death by a South Dakota jury. Rhines spent the next twenty-seven years on death row awaiting execution. In 2019 Rhines's attorneys appealed the case to the US Supreme Court on the grounds that jurors sentenced Rhines to death rather than life in prison because he was a homosexual. The attorneys based their appeal on the fact that after the trial several members of the jury admitted that Rhines's sexual orientation played a key role in their deliberations. According to an article on the website Vox, "One said that the jury knew that 'he was a homosexual and thought that he shouldn't be able to spend his life with men in prison.' Another recalled a fellow juror's statement that 'if he's gay, we'd be sending him where he wants to go if we voted for' life imprisonment. A third juror recalled 'lots of discussion of homosexuality. There was a lot of disgust.'"

Despite the jurors' confession, the Supreme Court refused to hear the case. Rhines was executed by lethal injection on November 4, 2019.

Quoted in Ian Millhiser, "Anti-Gay Prejudice May Have Driven Jurors to Sentence a Man to Death. His Execution Is Today," Vox, November 4, 2019. www.vox.com.

---

the Movement Advancement Project revealed that 3.4 percent of non-LGBTQ adults in the United States are incarcerated, compared to 8 percent of LGBTQ adults.

The difference is even more significant when it comes to transgender people and transgender people of color, according to the Justice Department's Bureau of Justice Statistics. Sixteen percent of all transgender people have been incarcerated at some time in their lives, including more than 20 percent of transgender women and almost half of all black transgender individuals. In comparison, only 5 percent of the total US population has been incarcerated at some point in their lives.

LGBTQ individuals may also face bias from lawyers, judges, and jury members who let their personal prejudices influence them.

And those who are found guilty of a crime are frequently mistreated by prison staff and fellow inmates once they are incarcerated. Gay and bisexual boys in juvenile detention facilities are almost eleven times more likely than straight boys to be sexually assaulted, as reported by the Center for American Progress and the Movement Advancement Project. Other studies reveal that LGBTQ inmates are disproportionately placed in solitary confinement and are more likely to face harsh treatment by staff than other prisoners.

Transgender inmates encounter even greater challenges. They are often placed in facilities that do not conform to their gender identity. This means that, in many cases, transgender men are sent to female prisons and transgender women are sent to male prisons, which endangers their safety. In fact, according to a National Center for Transgender Equality survey, transgender inmates are ten times as likely to be sexually assaulted by their fellow inmates and five times as likely to be sexually assaulted by prison staff as other prisoners. For instance, Sophia Brooks, a transgender woman, was placed in a male prison even though she had been physically transitioning for three years and had noticeable female attributes. She recounted being raped by other inmates, strip-searched by guards who mocked her during the process, and held for extended periods in solitary confinement for her own protection. Other transgender women report being forced to shower in front of male inmates, having their genitalia examined by nonmedical prison personnel, and being verbally and physically assaulted by guards and other inmates. In addition, transgender inmates are routinely denied medical care related to transitioning, such as hormone therapy.

Bias toward the LGBTQ community is still a part of American life. Discrimination against LGBTQ people negatively affects multiple aspects of their lives. That is why Olympic gold medalist and LGBTQ activist Megan Rapinoe says, "We're coming so far as a society, but we still have so far to go."[36]

> "We're coming so far as a society, but we still have so far to go."[36]
>
> —Megan Rapinoe, an Olympic gold medalist and LGBTQ activist

CHAPTER FOUR

Violence and Hate Crimes

In 2019 a man shouting homophobic slurs attacked Dazjuan Starr, a twenty-one-year-old gay man, in a New York City subway station. The assailant beat Starr with a hammer and then shoved him onto the tracks. Starr was able to climb to safety before he could be struck by a train. He suffered only minor injuries, but many other LGBTQ people have sustained serious—and sometimes fatal—injuries due to anti-LGBTQ violence. Gay men and transgender women of color, in particular, are frequent targets of hateful acts.

What Is a Hate Crime?

The assault on Starr was a hate crime. Hate crimes are crimes committed against a person or property and motivated by prejudice based on race, religion, ethnicity, gender, sexual orientation, or gender identity. Hate crimes include, but are not limited to, the desecration of public and private property, physical assaults, bomb and arson threats and attacks, and mass shootings. Under federal law, hate crimes are felonies. Felonies are the most serious crimes a person can commit. A felony conviction usually results in a long jail or prison sentence. Sometimes punishment also includes a fine and permanent loss of freedoms. According to the Federal Bureau of Investigation, out of a total of 7,120 hate crimes committed in 2018, 1,347 were directed at LGBTQ individuals. This translates to 18.5 percent of all hate crimes, which is a disproportionately large number considering that LGBTQ individuals make up only about 4.5 percent of the US population. Many of these crimes are quite vicious. In 2019, for example, twenty-four LGBTQ people were killed in violent attacks. Moreover, anti-LGBTQ hate crimes have been increasing in number. Between 2017 and 2018, hate crimes directed against the LGBTQ community, in general, increased by almost 6 percent. Hate crimes targeting transgender individuals, specifically, grew from 119 to 168 attacks, which is a 42 percent rise.

As disturbing as these statistics are, they may be low. For a variety of reasons, anti-LGBTQ hate crimes may be underreported. In some cases, police officers do not classify or report anti-LGBTQ crimes as hate crimes due to their own personal bias. In other instances, victims do not report a crime because they feel like law enforcement personnel will not support them. Other individuals shy away from reporting an incident because they do not want to reveal their sexual orientation or gender identity out of fear of being publicly outed. As Robin Maril, the associate legal director of the Human Rights Campaign, notes, "To the extent that we don't have universal protections from discrimination on the basis of employment, housing, and public accommodations, if someone comes forward to report a hate crime they could also be officially outing themselves as LGBTQ. In a smaller or rural community, that outing could result in an eviction or loss of a job."[37]

> "If someone comes forward to report a hate crime they could also be officially outing themselves as LGBTQ. In a smaller or rural community, that outing could result in an eviction or loss of a job."[37]
>
> —Robin Maril, the associate legal director of the Human Rights Campaign

Vandalism

Vandalizing property associated with the LGBTQ community is one way that bigoted individuals express their hatred and prejudice. Rainbow items, which are a symbol of gay pride, are frequent targets of anti-LGBTQ vandalism. In 2019 rainbow flags displayed outside private homes, stores, and public buildings were defaced, stolen, or set on fire in California, Iowa, New York, Utah, and Vermont, among other places. That same year, motorcyclists in New Mexico vandalized a newly painted rainbow crosswalk created in honor of Albuquerque Pride Week. Posters, billboards, and murals are also prime targets. For instance, in 2018 at least ten employee-designed LGBTQ pride posters displayed in the elevators at Amazon's Seattle, Washington, headquarters were defaced. Other posters displayed in a New York City subway station featuring soccer player Megan Rapinoe, the openly gay captain of the US Women's National Team, were vandalized with anti-LGBTQ slurs degrading Rapinoe.

Other forms of public art have also been defiled by homophobes and transphobes. In 2019 a vandal spray-painted blue mustaches on a mural in Dallas, Texas, honoring Sylvia

Supporters at a 2018 pride parade in San Francisco hold a banner denouncing hate against the LGBTQ community. In 2018 nearly 20 percent of all hate crimes targeted LGBTQ individuals.

Rivera and Marsha P. Johnson, transgender activists and veterans of the Stonewall Inn rebellion. That same year, in Tulsa, Oklahoma, a mural honoring gay playwright and Oklahoma native Lynn Riggs was covered with anti-LGBTQ slurs.

Churches, community centers, gender-neutral restrooms, and stores associated with the LGBTQ community have also felt the sting of hate crimes. In a number of incidents, their walls, windows, and doors have been tagged with vile messages and images, and in some cases, property has been destroyed. In one incident that occurred in 2019, pew cushions in a gay-friendly Connecticut church were slashed open, and the front door was defaced. The perpetrator told the police that he vandalized the church because he believed "the pastor and the church as a whole were supporting and pushing the LGBT agenda."[38]

Across the country in Las Vegas, the LGBTQ Center of Southern Nevada was vandalized twice in a three-month period in 2019. The first time, a palm tree adjacent to the building's entrance was set on fire in an attempt to burn down the building. The next time, the word *fag* was spray-painted in large letters across the building's front door. These types of incidents anger, frustrate, and often demoralize LGBTQ community members, but, generally, they do not intimidate them. Indeed, a spokesperson for the LGBTQ Center of Southern Nevada responded to the second attack on that establishment by posting the following on Facebook: "We woke up today like any other day, but on this day we're met with a reminder as to why we are still needed. The second act of vandalism to our Center in three months. Hatred will not stop us."[39]

Assaults

Some individuals have moved from vandalism to physically assaulting LGBTQ people. In 2018 alone, there were 478 cases of assaults. These ranged from simple assaults to attacks with deadly weapons. In many cases LGBTQ people are assaulted by someone they know, such as a coworker, family member, neighbor, or landlord. According to the New York City Anti-Violence

Anti-LGBTQ Hate Crimes Worldwide

Anti-LGBTQ hate crimes are a huge problem in many nations. According to a 2019 report by the Regional Information Network on Violence Against LGBTI (the I stands for intersex) People in Latin America and the Caribbean, approximately 4 LGBTQ people are murdered daily in that region. It reports that between 2014 and 2019, a total of 1,300 LGBTQ people were killed in the region, with 90 percent of the crimes occurring in Colombia, Honduras, and Mexico. In 2017 alone, 435 LGBTQ people were victims of fatal hate crimes in Brazil.

Hate crimes committed against LGBTQ people are also common in other regions of the world. In some nations, homophobia is condoned—and even encouraged—by the government, which helps to legitimize hate crimes. Homosexuality is a crime in seventy countries. In some of these countries, such as Afghanistan, Iran, Nigeria, Saudi Arabia, Senegal, Sudan, Uganda, and Zimbabwe, homosexuality is punishable by life in prison or even death. In fact, Amnesty International estimates that five thousand homosexual men and women have been executed in Iran since 1979.

Project, which tracks nationwide violence against LGBTQ people, 57 percent of LGBTQ people who experience anti-LGBTQ assaults know their assailant. In 2019, for instance, a gay couple in Ohio was shot at, called homophobic slurs, and had their car turned over and burned by a homophobic neighbor. "We shouldn't have to go through this kind of stuff," Nathan Paris, one of the victims, told the news media. "We're not bothering nobody. We're keeping to ourselves. We don't harass anyone. We don't bother anyone. We're just ourselves. That's all we are."[40]

In a 2018 case, Blaze Bernstein, a nineteen-year-old openly gay college student, was stabbed twenty times by a former high school classmate because of Bernstein's sexual orientation. Bernstein's bleeding body was left in a Southern California park, where he died from his injuries. After the murder, police found evidence on the assailant's computer, cell phone, and social media page revealing his hatred of LGBTQ people.

Samuel Woodward (pictured) leaves the courtroom during his murder trial in 2018. Woodard was charged with killing his former high school classmate, Blaze Bernstein, because of Bernstein's sexual orientation.

Although not as frequent, assaults by strangers are still quite common. These account for 43 percent of all anti-LGBTQ assaults. LGBTQ individuals are often targeted because of their actions, appearance, or because they are seen entering or exiting a facility associated with the LGBTQ community. "Gay people think about when to hold hands or kiss goodbye in public. Sometimes, it will be a matter of safety. The fact that straight couples don't have to think about these questions is a reminder of difference,"[41] explains Rose Saxe, the senior staff attorney for the LGBT & HIV Project of the American Civil Liberties Union (ACLU).

In Washington in 2019, a gay couple holding hands near a taco truck stand, for example, were attacked by four strangers. According to witnesses, the attackers hurled homophobic slurs at the victims.

> "Gay people think about when to hold hands or kiss goodbye in public. Sometimes, it will be a matter of safety. The fact that straight couples don't have to think about these questions is a reminder of difference."[41]
>
> —Rose Saxe, the senior staff attorney for the American Civil Liberties Union's LGBT & HIV Project

Then they punched and kicked one of the gay men, who suffered a concussion and broken ribs. Similarly, four men targeted and beat another gay couple as the couple walked hand in hand in Austin, Texas. As a result, both men were hospitalized.

Targeting Transgender Women

Some of the most horrific attacks target transgender women of color. They are increasingly the objects of hate crimes that result in severe injuries or death. According to the Human Rights Campaign, between 2013 and 2017, over one hundred transgender people were murdered in the United States. According to the Alliance for Full Acceptance, a transgender advocacy group in South Carolina, "We are at a crisis point that demands the nation's attention. At this moment, there is no sense of peace or security for our transgender community—and there won't be until their lives are truly respected and valued by society."[42]

The main targets of these attacks are transgender women of color. Attacks on black and Hispanic transgender women have become so common that the American Medical Association and the Human Rights Campaign call it a national epidemic. Of the twenty-four fatal attacks on LGBTQ people in 2019, twenty-one were against transgender women of color. As with other anti-LGBTQ hate crimes, these incidents may be underreported. This is because some victims are not identified as transgender by the police or by family members who refuse to acknowledge the victim's gender identity.

Although there is no documented reason why transgender women of color are disproportionately the victims of fatal attacks, social scientists theorize that it is due to the intersection of racism, sexism, homophobia, and transphobia. Among recent crimes against transgender women of color is the murder of Muhlaysia

> "We are at a crisis point that demands the nation's attention. At this moment, there is no sense of peace or security for our transgender community—and there won't be until their lives are truly respected and valued by society."[42]
>
> —The Alliance for Full Acceptance, a transgender advocacy group in South Carolina

Booker. She was found shot to death on a Dallas street in May 2019, a month after a video of her being beaten by a mob at an apartment complex went viral. Another is the murder of Bee Love Slater, who was found burned beyond recognition in her car in Florida. Investigators said that it was one of the most brutal crimes they had ever seen.

What makes these crimes even more disturbing is the use and acceptance of a legal tactic known as the gay/trans panic defense, which seeks to excuse attacks on transgender and gay individuals by blaming the victim. Under the gay/trans panic defense, defendants claim they acted in a state of temporary panic or insanity when they found out the victim was transgender or gay. According to Richard Saenz, a lawyer at Lambda Legal, an LGBTQ civil rights organization, "It assumes that this person [the victim] was hiding or trying to be deceptive in some way. And when their sexual orientation or gender identity was discovered, the response was reasonable, even to the point of death."[43]

The gay/trans panic defense is a controversial tactic that plays on the personal prejudices and sympathies of members of the jury; it is condemned by many legal organizations, including the American Bar Association. In fact, that organization issued a resolution prohibiting the use of this defense in 2013, calling it "legally sanctioned discrimination against one's sexual orientation and gender identity."[44] As of January 2020, nine states have banned the gay/trans panic defense. Nevertheless, the tactic is still used in other states as a way for defendants to obtain a lesser sentence or avoid conviction entirely.

Mass Violence

The gay/trans panic defense is not a suitable defense tactic for perpetrators of mass violence, but that does not deter some individuals from committing or attempting to commit mass violence against LGBTQ people and institutions. Mass shootings, bombings, and arson are among the types of large-scale attacks that

Transgender Day of Remembrance

Transgender Day of Remembrance is a worldwide annual event that honors and memorializes transgender people who were killed in antitransgender violence. At the same time, it raises public awareness of the challenges and dangers transgender people face. According to Gwendolyn Ann Smith, a transgender activist and the founder of the holiday,

> Transgender Day of Remembrance seeks to highlight the losses we face due to anti-transgender bigotry and violence. I am no stranger to the need to fight for our rights, and the right to simply exist is first and foremost. With so many seeking to erase transgender people—sometimes in the most brutal ways possible—it is vitally important that those we lose are remembered, and that we continue to fight for justice.
>
> The holiday is observed each year on November 20 in more than 185 cities in more than twenty countries. To honor victims, the names of transgender individuals who were killed during the previous year are read aloud. Candlelight vigils and marches are usually held, and money is raised through various events to support transgender causes. Food drives, film screenings, art shows, and church services are also often part of the event.

Quoted in GLAAD, "Transgender Day of Remembrance Nov 20." www.glaad.org.

---

have been committed against LGBTQ individuals and institutions. A mass shooting on June 12, 2016, at Pulse nightclub in Orlando, Florida, was the deadliest attack on the LGBTQ community in US history. The nightclub was a popular place for Orlando's LGBTQ community to dance and socialize. The shooter was a man named Omar Mateen. According to Mateen's father, Mateen may have targeted the nightclub after he became angered when he saw two men kissing outside a market weeks prior to the shooting. There were over three hundred people inside the club at the time of the attack. Before the police shot and killed

Posters feature images of the forty-nine victims of a mass shooting at Pulse nightclub in Orlando, Florida. On June 12, 2016, a man targeted the nightclub after he became angered seeing two men kissing weeks earlier.

Mateen, he murdered forty-nine people and wounded fifty-three others, many seriously. Many of the survivors say they still suffer from post-traumatic stress disorder as a result of the trauma they endured.

The attack on the Pulse nightclub was not an isolated event. Just a few days after the massacre, a Los Angeles man was arrested for carrying explosives that he planned to detonate at the city's gay pride parade. Other mass attacks have also been thwarted by law enforcement. Would-be attackers sometimes post threats against the LGBTQ community on social media before acting upon them. Or they talk freely about their plans to others. Tips from concerned citizens who see the posts or interact with the attacker help alert law enforcement to impending danger. In 2019, for instance, Ralph Perkins of Tampa, Florida, posted the following message online: "I like to take a gun [and] I like to wipe the whole gay community out in Tampa and then kill myself. That's going to be my ultimate present to Tampa."[45] The police received a tip about the post and arrested Perkins before he could act on his plan. Similarly, an attack on a popular Las Vegas gay bar was thwarted in 2019 when law enforcement learned about a plan by Connor Climo to attack the venue. When police searched his house, they found caches of ammunition and assault weapons, bulletproof armor, bomb-making materials, explosives, and a journal with hand-drawn pictures related to his plan.

The Long-Term Effects

The ever-present threat of anti-LGBTQ violence produces extreme stress in the lives of many LGBTQ individuals and their loved ones. Living with prolonged stress has been shown to negatively affect a person's physical and emotional health, leading to depression, anxiety, heart disease, headaches, and other ailments. Plus, it is demoralizing to be targeted simply because of who you are. Such threats and attacks foment a sense of otherness among LGBTQ people, which is why, in a June 2016 speech memorializing Pulse nightclub shooting victims, Barack Obama insisted, "We have to end discrimination and violence against our brothers and sisters who are in the LGBT community."[46]

CHAPTER FIVE

What the Future Holds

As of mid-2020 there was no federal law that explicitly protects individuals from discrimination based on sexual orientation or gender identity. LGBTQ people must depend on individual state and city laws for protection. Yet these laws vary widely. According to Chad Griffin, the president of the Human Rights Campaign, "If an LGBTQ couple drove from Maine to California today, their legal rights and civil rights protections could change more than 20 times at state borders and city lines."[47]

Twenty-eight states and the District of Columbia have laws that prohibit discrimination based on a person's sexual orientation and gender identity. Most of these states have also banned the gay/trans panic defense and the use of conversion therapy for LGBTQ youths and have enacted antibullying rules that protect LGBTQ students. Twenty-two states do not have anti-LGBTQ discrimination laws. In some of these states, the laws actually sanction discrimination against LGBTQ people. For instance, Missouri and South Dakota have laws that prohibit school districts from protecting LGBTQ students from bullying. Arkansas, North Carolina, and Tennessee have laws preventing the passage or enforcement of municipal workplace nondiscrimination laws. Adding to the problem, lawmakers in many states have been trying to pass new anti-LGBTQ laws.

Legislators in Texas introduced nineteen anti-LGBTQ laws in 2019 alone. Although none of the Texas bills were enacted, the trend is upsetting.

Lacking national protections, LGBTQ activists, advocacy groups, and their supporters have been working to get a bill known as the Equality Act passed. It explicitly bans discrimination based on sexual orientation and gender identity, thereby giving LGBTQ people the same rights as other Americans. The US House of Representatives passed the bill in May 2019. However, President Trump opposes the bill, and Majority Leader Mitch McConnell has refused to bring it up for a vote in the Senate. LGBTQ activists have not given up on the bill but are realistic about its chances of being taken up by the Senate. Therefore, they are also trying to get pro-LGBTQ laws enacted in the states that lack these regulations. This is not an easy task. Politics and religious exemption laws play an important role in how people view and treat the LGBTQ community.

> "If an LGBTQ couple drove from Maine to California today, their legal rights and civil rights protections could change more than 20 times at state borders and city lines."[47]
>
> —Chad Griffin, the president of the Human Rights Campaign

The Effect of Politics

Whether or not the Equality Act or state laws that expand LGBTQ rights are passed depends, to a great degree, on politics. Politics also influences the way Americans view and treat LGBTQ individuals. Generally, people who identify as liberals support the Democratic Party, which mostly favors protecting and expanding the rights of LGBTQ people. People who identify as conservatives usually back the Republican Party, which mostly does not favor broader LGBTQ protections. A 2019 Pew Research Center poll found that 88 percent of respondents who identify as liberal Democrats support same-sex marriage, compared to 36 percent of those who identify as conservative Republicans. Similarly, 76 percent of liberal Democrats who responded to an earlier Gallup poll support the Equality Act, in contrast to 29 percent of conservative Republicans.

From 2008 to 2016, while Democrat Barack Obama was president, a number of pro-LGBTQ policies were enacted nationwide. These included legalizing same-sex marriage, reversing the ban on LGBTQ people openly serving in the military, giving federal contractors protections against discrimination on the basis of sexual orientation and gender identity, supporting federal protections against the bullying of LGBTQ students in schools, and supporting the rights of transgender people to use public restrooms that match their gender identity. Moreover, the administration's support for the LGBTQ community made identifying as LGBTQ more acceptable.

LGBTQ activists have been working to get a bill known as the Equality Act passed. President Trump and Senate Majority Leader Mitch McConnell (pictured) oppose the bill.

When Donald Trump, a Republican, took office in 2017, his administration proceeded to try to undo many pro-LGBTQ rights policies. "We've gone from a position where LGBT people are protected to one where we're not,"[48] says James Esseks, the director of the ACLU's LGBT & HIV Project.

> "We've gone from a position where LGBT people are protected to one where we're not."[48]
>
> —James Esseks, the director of the ACLU's LGBT & HIV Project

Since taking office, the Trump administration has issued executive orders, supported policies, delivered legal challenges, and made judicial and other personnel appointments unfavorable to the LGBTQ community. For example, in 2017 the Trump administration tried to reinstate a ban on transgender people openly serving in the military. After pushback by the courts, LGBTQ advocacy groups, and military experts, a compromise was reached. Currently, troops are allowed to identify as transgender but must use bathroom and sleeping facilities and wear uniforms that conform to their biological sex, among other conditions.

In other actions, the Trump administration threw out the Obama administration's guidance on protecting transgender students who are denied access to bathrooms and locker rooms based on their gender identity and removed protections for transgender prisoners. The latter allows the Bureau of Prisons to use the sex designated on a transgender inmate's birth certificate to determine placement, thereby increasing possible exposure to sexual assault. Trump also proposed a rule that would remove health care protections for transgender people who are insured under the Affordable Care Act.

In addition, the Trump administration has turned to the courts to support its agenda, filing court briefs making it legal to discriminate against transgender people in the workplace. In one such case, the Justice Department argued that a Michigan funeral home could fire a transgender woman because she wanted to dress in women's clothing. In 2018 a federal circuit court ruled that the woman was the victim of unlawful discrimination. However, the

Pete Buttigieg (pictured) is an openly gay former presidential candidate. During his campaign, he often noted how hostile the Trump administration policies have been to LGBTQ people.

case was being appealed to the US Supreme Court. According to Pete Buttigieg, the former mayor of South Bend, Indiana, and an openly gay former candidate for the Democratic nomination for president in 2020, "Every policy turn we've seen out of this administration has been hostile to LGBTQ people."[49]

The Long-Term Impact

Other anti-LGBTQ actions involve the appointment of conservative judges and government officials. According to Lambda Legal, in Trump's first three years in office, he appointed fifty federal circuit court judges, one-third of whom have a documented history of anti-LGBTQ bias. These judges rule on appeals of cases decided by lower courts and are one step below the Supreme Court justices. Lawrence Vandyke is one of these appointees. Vandyke received a "nonqualified" rating from the American Bar Association, partially out of concern that he would not be fair to LGBTQ people. Gregory Katsas, a former deputy White House counsel for Trump, is another judicial appointee. Lambda Legal reports that as deputy White House counsel, Katsas promoted the transgender military ban and opposed protecting transgender students from discrimination. The organization also reports that another appointee, Steven Menashi, opposed the legalization of same-sex marriage and the repeal of Don't Ask, Don't Tell.

Since Federal Circuit Court judges are appointed for life, they have many years to move their conservative anti-LGBTQ agenda forward. As Sharon McGowan, the legal director of Lambda Legal, explains, "When it comes to judges, we're looking at 20, 30 or 40 years of impact that will extend far beyond however long this administration lasts."[50]

Religious Exemption Policies

One rationale used to justify treating LGBTQ people differently is based on a conservative interpretation of the First Amendment of the US Constitution. It guarantees all Americans freedom to practice any religion they chose. Many conservatives argue that if a law challenges a person's or organization's religious beliefs or practices, being required to comply with that law violates their First Amendment right to religious freedom. They maintain that they are exempt from following such laws, even if doing so impacts the rights of others. Many liberals, on the other hand, contend that the First Amendment does not give anyone the right to discriminate.

The Trump administration backs the conservative point of view. It has thrown its support behind state laws allowing foster care and adoption agencies, homeless shelters, businesses, employers, and health care professionals to discriminate against LGBTQ people and others based on their religious beliefs. Indeed, Press Secretary Sarah Huckabee Sanders told reporters in 2017 that the Trump administration supported the rights of businesses to post signs stating they refuse to serve LGBTQ people. That same year, the president signed an executive order directing the federal government to enforce protections for religious freedom.

Approximately twenty-one states have enacted laws that essentially legalize discrimination against LGBTQ people on the basis of religious freedom. According to Human Rights Watch, the religious exemption laws

> send a signal that the state governments enacting them accept and even embrace the dangerous and harmful notion that discrimination against LGBT people is a legitimate demand of both conscience and religion. Particularly in states that lack any underlying laws prohibiting discrimination against LGBT people, many of the laws are not "exemptions" so much as a license to discriminate.[51]

These laws vary in scope. Some focus on public accommodations, allowing businesses like florists and caterers to refuse to provide goods and services for same-sex weddings or other LGBTQ events. Others permit child welfare agencies, health care providers, housing providers, employers, businesses that serve the public, and educational institutions to refuse service to LGBTQ people and other groups. Mississippi's Religious Accommodations Act, for example, permits businesses to deny service to LGBTQ people, lets employers fire LGBTQ workers because of their sexual orientation and gender identity, and prohibits transgender students from wearing clothes that do not match the gender they were assigned at birth, among other provisions. Laws in Alabama, Michigan, North Dakota, South Dakota, Texas, and Virginia allow adoption and foster care agencies to refuse to place children with LGBTQ parents due to the agencies' moral or religious objections. Erin Busk-Sutton experienced this form of discrimination firsthand when she was turned away from a foster care agency in Michigan because she is a lesbian. She says it was "the worst experience of my life, being told by a stranger that I wouldn't be a good mother, essentially."[52]

A number of cases have been brought before the courts related to whether owners of public accommodations (stores, restaurants, bars, etc.) can deny services to LGBTQ people based on religious freedom. In one famous case, the owner of the Masterpiece Cakeshop in Colorado refused to provide a custom-made cake for a same-sex couple's wedding. As a devout Christian, he said, he believes that same-sex marriages are immoral. He argued that providing the couple with a cake violated his First Amendment rights. The couple, who said that the experience made them feel degraded, challenged the baker in court, alleging discrimination.

Religious Leaders Speak Out

Although many religious leaders and groups vigorously support religious exemption policies that threaten the rights of LGBTQ people, a number of progressive religious leaders have voiced their opposition to these policies. In fact, when the Masterpiece Cakeshop case went before the US Supreme Court, thirteen hundred religious leaders—representing about a half million congregants of approximately fifty different faiths—sent a message to the court saying that religion should not be used to support discrimination or harm to others. The message stated,

> It is both morally wrong and not constitutionally required to permit blanket discrimination in the public marketplace for goods and services based on the personal religious beliefs of merchants with respect to same-sex couples' rights and relationships. . . . [We] believe that, to the contrary, public accommodation laws should be applied on the basis of religiously neutral principles of equal protection under the law.

Some religious leaders have also spoken out in support of the Equality Act. Before the US House of Representatives passed the act, an interfaith group consisting of Christian, Hindu, Jewish, and Muslim religious leaders rallied in front of the United Methodist Building on Capitol Hill in support of the bill. In addition, seventy-one religious groups signed a letter supporting the bill.

Quoted in Reconstructing Judaism, "Joint Filing Opposing Anti-LGBTQ Religious Exemptions in Supreme Court Case," October 30, 2017. www.reconstructingjudaism.org.

Pictured is the owner of a bakery speaking to the press outside of the US Supreme Court. In 2018 the court sided with the owner on his right to refuse to make a custom-made cake for a same-sex couple, citing his religious beliefs.

Colorado has antidiscrimination laws that require public businesses to serve all customers, no matter their sexual orientation or gender identity. The Colorado Civil Rights Board and a state court ruled in favor of the couple, based on the state's antidiscrimination law. However, after several appeals, the case reached the US Supreme Court in 2018. The court sided with the baker, saying the prior decisions showed antireligious bias against him.

Advocating for LGBTQ Rights

With the expansion of religious exemption policies and the dismantling of some pro-LGBTQ policies, LGBTQ advocacy organizations have their work cut out for them. They, as well as supportive individuals, organizations, and businesses, are working to raise public awareness of LGBTQ issues, gain greater acceptance for LGBTQ people, preserve pro-LGBTQ policies, and get the Equality Act passed. The Human Rights Campaign is among these organizations. It advocates for the rights of LGBTQ people, and other groups, such as GLAAD, try to ensure that LGBTQ people and issues are accurately represented in the media.

They are not alone in their fight. More than five hundred organizations and businesses have publicly declared their support of the Equality Act. These organizations include the ACLU, the American Medical Association, and the American Bar Association as well as businesses such as Apple, Google, and IBM. Some interfaith groups and religious leaders have also lent their support, as have celebrities like Taylor Swift, Bella Thorn, and Sally Field, among others. In fact, Swift organized a petition supporting the act, which she urged all her fans to sign.

Celebrities Who Support LGBTQ Rights

A large number of celebrities have publicly thrown their support behind the LGBTQ rights movement. They have spoken out, started petitions, lobbied lawmakers, contributed their time and money, and established organizations that support protecting and expanding the rights of LGBTQ people. Lady Gaga, for example, started the Born This Way Foundation, an antibullying organization that works to protect LGBTQ students. Similarly, Miley Cyrus founded the Happy Hippy Foundation, which is dedicated to helping homeless LGBTQ youth. Cyrus also partnered with Instagram to help transgender people share their stories.

Taylor Swift is another strong advocate for LGBTQ rights. She was the 2020 winner of GLAAD's Vanguard Award, which is presented to celebrities who have made a significant effort to promote LGBTQ rights. Previous Vanguard Award winners include Brad Pitt, Beyoncé, Jay-Z, Jim Parsons, Laverne Cox, and Ellen DeGeneres, among others.

Other celebrities who have taken a public stand in support of the LGBTQ community include Anne Hathaway, whose brother is openly gay; Ellen Page, who came out as gay in 2014; Kerry Washington, Daniel Radcliffe, Pink, and Justin Timberlake. Athletes, too, have also voiced their support. These individuals include pitcher Justin Verlander of the Houston Astros; retired hockey player Sean Avery of the New York Rangers; and former football player and Hall of Famer Michael Ervin of the Dallas Cowboys, just to name a few.

Support and Pride

Whereas some groups and individuals are working to gain equal rights for LGBTQ people, other organizations provide services that help them to feel valued. Some of these organizations focus on the needs of LGBTQ youth. They offer counseling and suicide prevention services, social activities, and school programs, which help young people to understand that they are not abnormal, sinful, or alone. For example, GLSEN sponsors school clubs and youth summits. These clubs and summits give LGBTQ students the chance to support and socialize with each other and with non-LGBTQ students who support the LGBTQ community. PFLAG also has programs aimed at making schools safe for LGBTQ students, as well as programs that help LGBTQ people and their families deal with the issues they face. Other groups, such as the Gay and Lesbian Association of Choruses, sponsor choral groups comprised of LGBTQ singers as well as special youth choruses. Participants socialize, develop their artistic skills, and feel valued while singing in concerts and festivals throughout the world.

> "To me Pride means that I am worthy of love, despite what I learned growing up."[53]
>
> —Steve, a member of the LGBTQ community

Pride activities, which occur across the globe during June (Pride Month), are dedicated to making LGBTQ people feel valued and proud. As Steve, a member of the LGBTQ community, explains, "To me Pride means that I am worthy of love, despite what I learned growing up."[53]

Pride events bring hundreds of thousands of LGBTQ people and their supporters together to celebrate the LGBTQ community and how far they have come. Activities include concerts, festivals, workshops, and small and huge parades. In 2019 an estimated 2 million people took part in New York City's pride parade. Pride events are not only fun, though. Being part of a supportive community lets LGBTQ people know that they are not alone and that they are respected. It helps them to face the future, no matter what it may hold.

SOURCE NOTES

Introduction: Many Challenges

1. Quoted in Anna Blackshaw, "Yes We're Queer: LGBTQ Youth Speak Out," *Indy Week*, May 2, 2012. https://indyweek.com.
2. Quoted in Blackshaw, "Yes We're Queer."
3. Quoted in Susan Kuklin, *Beyond Magenta*. Somerville, MA: Candlewick, 2014, p. 95.
4. Quoted in Ryan Richard Thoreson, *"All We Want Is Equality": Religious Exemptions and Discrimination Against LGBT People in the United States*. New York: Human Rights Watch, 2018. www.hrw.org.

Chapter One: A Troubling History

5. Quoted in Linas Alsenas, *Gay America*. New York: Harry N. Abrams, 2008, p. 55.
6. Quoted in Alsenas, *Gay America*, p. 43.
7. Quoted in Lillian Faderman, *The Gay Revolution*. New York: Simon & Schuster, 2015, p. 177.
8. Quoted in *Democracy Now!*, "Stonewall Riots 40th Anniversary: A Look Back at the Uprising That Launched the Modern Gay Rights Movement," June 26, 2009. www.democracynow.org.
9. Quoted in *Democracy Now!*, "Stonewall Riots 40th Anniversary."
10. Quoted in Rick Unger, "What Was Obama Talking About When He Cited the Historical References of 'Seneca Falls and Selma and Stonewall'?," *Forbes*, January 2, 2013. www.forbes.com.
11. Quoted in David E. Newton, *LGBT Youth Issues Today*. Santa Barbara, CA: ABC-CLIO, 2014, p. 31.
12. Quoted in *Times* Staff, "Faces of Gay Marriage: Tampa Bay Couples Talk About Why They've Tied the Knot," *Tampa Bay Times*, January 6, 2015. www.tampabay.com.

13. Quoted in Shane M. Stahl, "Exclusive: Entertainment Icon Lynda Carter 'Wonders' Why Equality Isn't Yet Law of the Land," Freedom for All Americans, October 9, 2018. www.freedomforallamericans.org.

Chapter Two: Growing Up LGBTQ Is Not Easy

14. Quoted in Dan Savage and Terry Miller, eds., *It Gets Better*. New York: Plume, 2012, p. 118.
15. Quoted in Savage and Miller, *It Gets Better*, p. 11.
16. Quoted in Savage and Miller, *It Gets Better*, p. 96.
17. Quoted in Savage and Miller, *It Gets Better*, p. 211.
18. Quoted in Marissa Higgins, "LBGT Students Are Not Safe at School," *The Atlantic*, October 18, 2016. www.theatlantic.com.
19. Quoted in Higgins, "LBGT Students Are Not Safe at School."
20. Quoted in Newton, *LGBT Youth Issues Today*, p. 92.
21. Quoted in Elly Belle, "What High School Is Like for Transgender Students," *Teen Vogue*, September 15, 2018. www.teenvogue.com.
22. Quoted in Savage and Miller, *It Gets Better*, p. 264.
23. Quoted in Savage and Miller, *It Gets Better*, p. 51.
24. Quoted in Savage and Miller, *It Gets Better*, p. 96.
25. Quoted in James Michael Nichols, "A Survivor of Gay Conversion Therapy Shares His Chilling Story," *Huffington Post*, November 17, 2016. www.huffpost.com.
26. Quoted in Movement Advancement Project, "Unjust: How the Broken Criminal Justice System Fails LGBT People," Center for American Progress, February 2016, p. 34. www.lgbtmap.org.
27. Newton, *LGBT Youth Issues Today*, p. 106.

Chapter Three: The Long Reach of Discrimination

28. Quoted in Naomi Andu, "After Penalizing Gay Teacher, Mansfield ISD Awards Her $100,000, Plans Vote to Ban Sexual Orientation Discrimination," Texas Tribune, February 25, 2020. www.texastribune.org.
29. Quoted in Sejal Singh and Laura E. Durso, "Widespread Discrimination Continues to Shape LGBT People's Lives in Both Subtle and Significant Ways," Center for American Progress, May 2, 2017. www.americanprogress.org.

30. Nita, telephone interview with the author, February 28, 2020.
31. Quoted in Lou Chibbaro Jr., "Study Reveals LGBT Rental Housing Discrimination," *Washington Blade*, July 3, 2017. www.washingtonblade.com.
32. Quoted in Frank Bruni, "The Worst (and Best) Places to Be Gay in America," *New York Times*, August 25, 2017. www.nytimes.com.
33. Quoted in National Center for Transgender Equality, "Transgender People Share Stories of Prejudice and Stigma in Health Care," *National Center for Transgender Equality Blog*, July 29, 2019. https://transequality.org.
34. Quoted in Healthline, "The Discrimination LGBTQ People Still Face from Healthcare Providers." www.healthline.com.
35. Quoted in Movement Advancement Project, "Unjust," p. 22.
36. Quoted in Queer Culture Chats, "21 Best LGBT Quotes in Honor of Pride," June 4, 2018. https://queerculturechats.org.

Chapter Four: Violence and Hate Crimes

37. Quoted in Grace Hauk, "Anti-LGBTQ Hate Crimes Are Rising the FBI Says. But It Gets Worse," *USA Today*, July 1, 2019. www.usatoday.com.
38. Quoted in Diane Orson, "Vandalism at Connecticut Church Tied to Its Affirmation of LGBTQ Community," Connecticut Public Radio, July 8, 2019. www.wnpr.org.
39. Quoted in Gwendolyn Smith, "First Vandals Tried to Burn the LGBTQ Center Down. Now They've Left Anti-Gay Slurs on the Front Door," LGBTQ Nation, September 6, 2019. www.lgbtqnation.com.
40. Quoted in Alex Bollinger, "This Gay Couple's Neighbor Has Torched Their Car & Tried to Shoot Them. Police Won't Help Them," LGBTQ Nation, May 28, 2019. www.lgbtqnation.com.
41. Rose Saxe, "It's Always Been About Discrimination for LGBT People," *Speak Freely* (blog), American Civil Liberties Union, December 1, 2017. www.aclu.org.
42. Quoted in Trudy Ring, "These Are the Trans People Killed in 2019," *The Advocate*, May 22, 2019. www.advocate.com.
43. Quoted in Michael Gold, "'Gay Panic' Defenses Are Banned in N.Y. Murder Cases," *New York Times*, June 19, 2019. www.nytimes.com.

44. Alexandra Holden, "The Gay/Trans Panic Defense: What It Is, and How to End It," American Bar Association, July 10, 2019. www.americanbar.org.
45. Quoted in Trudy Ring, "Tampa Man Charged with Threatening to Wipe Out City's Gay Community," *The Advocate*, December 19, 2019. www.advocate.com.
46. Barack Obama, "In Full: President Obama's Speech in Orlando," Pink News, June 17, 2016. www.pinknews.co.uk.

Chapter Five: What the Future Holds

47. Quoted in Elliot Kozuch, "State Equality Index," *HRC Blog*, Human Rights Campaign, 2017. www.hrc.org.
48. Quoted in German Lopez, "Trump Promised to Be LGBTQ-Friendly. His First Year in Office Proved It Was a Giant Con," Vox, January 22, 2018. www.vox.com.
49. Quoted in Toluse Olorunnipa, "Trump, Who Cast Himself as Pro-LGBT, Is Now Under Fire from Democrats for Rolling Back Protections," *Washington Post*, May 31, 2019. www.washingtonpost.com.
50. Quoted in Asher Stockler, "With New Appointments, More than One-Third of Trump Appeals Judges Have Record of Anti-LGBT Bias," *Newsweek*, December 20, 2019. www.newsweek.com.
51. Thoreson, *"All We Want Is Equality."*
52. Quoted in Human Rights Watch, "United States: State Laws Threaten LGBT Equality," February 19, 2018. www.hrw.org.
53. Quoted in Robin Stevenson, *Pride: Celebrating Diversity & Community*. Victoria, Canada: Orca, 2016, p. 68.

ORGANIZATIONS AND WEBSITES

American Civil Liberties Union (ACLU)—www.aclu.org

The ACLU advocates for and defends the civil rights of all Americans. It has a large section on its website dealing with LGBTQ rights.

Center for American Progress
www.americanprogress.org

The Center for American Progress is a progressive institute that is dedicated to improving the lives of all Americans, including the LGBTQ community. It has more than three hundred articles on its website regarding LGBTQ issues.

GLAAD—www.glaad.org

GLAAD is a national organization that monitors media coverage of the LGBTQ community and works to increase public acceptance of LGBTQ people. It offers a wealth of information about all types of LGBTQ issues on its website.

GLSEN—www.glsen.org

GLSEN is a national organization dedicated to making schools safe for LGBTQ students. It sponsors student clubs and programs, training for educators, webinars, and workshops. Its website provides lesson plans for teachers, reports and information about laws and policies concerning LGBTQ students, and much more.

Human Rights Campaign—www.hrc.org

The Human Rights Campaign advocates for and defends the civil rights of LGBTQ people. It is the largest such organization in the United States. It provides articles, reports, news, videos, and all types of information regarding LGBTQ rights on its website.

National Center for Transgender Equality
https://transequality.org

The National Center for Transgender Equality advocates for the civil rights of transgender people. It offers a blog, articles, reports, graphics, and videos related to transgender rights and the challenges transgender people face.

PFLAG—https://pflag.org

With four hundred chapters and more than two hundred thousand members, PFLAG is the oldest and biggest support organization for LGBTQ people and their parents, families, and friends. PFLAG works to increase acceptance and respect of LGBTQ people among family members as well as the public. It offers seven scholarships and provides a blog, news, and articles on its website.

Trevor Project—www.thetrevorproject.org

The Trevor Project provides crisis intervention and suicide prevention services for LGBTQ youths and adults. It has a telephone hotline (1-866-488-7386) as well as counseling services via text and chat. It also offers resources for educators, suicide prevention resource materials, and articles regarding LGBTQ issues on its website.

FOR FURTHER RESEARCH

Books

Kathy Belge and Marke Bieschke, *Queer: The Ultimate LGBTQ Guide for Teens*. 2nd ed. Minneapolis: Zest, 2019.

Heidi C. Feldman, *LGBT Discrimination*. San Diego: ReferencePoint, 2019.

Duchess Harris, *LGBTQ Discrimination in America*. Minneapolis: Abdo, 2020.

Duchess Harris and Martha Lundin, *LGBTQ Rights and the Law*. Minneapolis: Abdo, 2020.

Sean Heather K. McGraw, *The Gay Liberation Movement: Before and After Stonewall*. New York: Rosen, 2019.

Pat Rarus, *The LGBT Rights Movement*. San Diego: ReferencePoint, 2019.

Internet Sources

Lucy Diavolo, "The United States Government's Anti-Gay Lavender Scare, Explained," *Teen Vogue*, April 26, 2019. www.teenvogue.com.

Infoplease Staff, "The American Gay Rights Movement: A Time Line," Infoplease, February 11. 2017. www.infoplease.com.

It Gets Better Project, "Stories." https://itgetsbetter.org.

Carolyn Jones, "Young, Gay and Living on the Street: LGBT Youth Face Increased Risk of Homelessness," EdSource, January 1, 2018. https://edsource.org.

Trudy Ring, "The Top LGBTQ Stories of the 2010s," *The Advocate*, December 31, 2019. www.advocate.com.

Ryan Richard Thoreson, *"All We Want Is Equality": Religious Exemptions and Discrimination Against LGBT People in the United States*. New York: Human Rights Watch, 2018. www.hrw.org.

INDEX

Note: Boldface page numbers indicate illustrations.

acquired immunodeficiency syndrome (AIDS) epidemic, 15–16
activism, 14–15, 62–63, 69
 See also Human Rights Campaign
Affordable Care Act, 57
Alabama, 60
alcohol abuse, 30
Alliance for Full Acceptance, 49
American Bar Association, 50, 58, 63
American Civil Liberties Union (ACLU), 63, 69
American Medical Association
 attacks on black and Hispanic transgender women and, 49
 code of ethics, 38
 conversion therapy and, 28
 support for Equality Act, 63
American Psychiatric Association, 28
Amnesty International, 47
androgynous, defined, 12
anti-vice groups, 9
Apple, 63
Arkansas, 54
assaults
 assailants known to victim, 47
 assailants not known to victim, 48–49
 mass violence, 50–53, **52**
 murders of transgender women of color, 49
 number of, in 2018, 46
 in school, 22
 sexual
  against homeless youth, 30
  against LGBTQ boys in juvenile detention facilities, 42
  against transgender individuals, 25–26, 42
  against transgender prison inmates, 42
 Transgender Day of Remembrance and, 51
 transgender women as targets, 49–50
Avery, Sean, 63

Bailey, Stacy, 33
Baker, Kaj, 36
Bernstein, Blaze, 47
Beyoncé, 63
bicurious, defined, 12
Bond, Pat, 9–10
Booker, Muhlaysia, 49–50
Born This Way Foundation, 63
Brooks, Sophia, 42
Brown, Khris, 22
Bryant, Anita, 14–15
bullying
 Born This Way Foundation and, 63
 online, 27, 36
 percentage of youth not reporting, 23–24
 percentage of youth whose reports were ignored, 24
 in school, 22, **22**
 state laws prohibiting schools from protecting LGBTQ students from, 54
 in workplace, 33–35
Bureau of Justice Statistics (Justice Department), 41
Busk-Sutton, Erin, 60

73

Buttigieg, Pete, 58, **58**

California, 14
CareerBuilder, 33
Caribbean, LGBTQ as victims of fatal hate crimes in, 47
Carter, Lynda, 19
Center for American Progress
  basic information about, 69
  percentage of LGBTQ adults incarcerated, 40–41
  sexual assault of LGBTQ boys in juvenile detention facilities, 42
  transgender individuals as targets of health care discrimination, 38
Chavez, Alexis, 38–39
churches, vandalism against gay-friendly, 46
cisgender, defined, 12
Civil Rights Act (1964), 11
Clinton, Bill, 16, **17**
closeted, 11
Colorado, 14, 60–62
coming out, 12, 14
conversion therapy, 28
Cornish, Queen, 23
Cox, Laverne, 63
criminal justice system discrimination
  incarceration rate of LGBTQ individuals, 40–41
  mistreatment in prison, 42
  police targeting of LGBTQ individuals, 39–40
  prejudicial jurors and court personnel, 41
  Trump administration and workplace discrimination against transgender individuals, 57–58
  Trump appointment of federal judges with anti-LGBTQ bias, 58–59
cyberbullying and harassment, 27, 36
Cyrus, Miley, 63

Defense of Marriage Act (1996), 16, 17
DeGeneres, Ellen, 63
Democratic Party, 55
Don't Ask, Don't Tell policy, 16, 19, 59
drug abuse, 30

education
  attitude and actions of teachers, 23, **25**
  Born This Way Foundation and, 63
  clubs at school, 23
  harassment, assaults, and bullying in school, 4, 20–23, **22**
  PFLAG services, 64
  school policies, 23–26
  state laws prohibiting schools from protecting LGBTQ students from bullying, 54
employment. *See* workplace discrimination
Equality Act (bill), 55, 61, 63
Equal Rights Center, 35–36
Ervin, Michael, 63
Esseks, James, 57

Faderman, Lillian, 14
Faire, Jheri, 18
family, 27–30
Farrow, Kelli, 38
Federal Bureau of Investigation, 43–44
Federal Fair Housing Act, 35
Field, Sally, 63
First Amendment (US Constitution), 59–62
Florida, mass shooting in, 51–52, **52**

Gallup polls, 55
Gay and Lesbian Association of Choruses, 64
Gay Straight Alliance, 23
gay/trans panic defense, 50
gender dysphoria, defined, 12
gender expression, defined, 12
gender fluid, defined, 12
GLAAD, 62–63, 69
GLSEN
  basic information about, 69
  percentage of youth not reporting bullying, 23–24
  percentage of youth who experienced cyberbullying, 27
  percentage of youth whose reports were ignored, 24
  services for LGBTQ youth, 64

skipping school by LGBTQ students, 23
Google, 63
Griffin, Chad, 54

Happy Hippy Foundation, 63
harassment
  online, 27, 36
  in school, 22, **22**
  sexual, of youth, 27
  in workplace, 33–35
Hardwick, Michael, 8
hate crimes
  described, 43
  global, 47
  reporting of, 44
  statistics, 44
  underreporting of, 44, 49
  use of gay/trans panic defense, 50
  vandalism as, 44–46
  See also assaults
Hathaway, Anne, 63
Hawaii, 14
health care discrimination, 38–39, 42, 57
homeless youth, 29–30, 63
homophobia, defined, 7
housing, 29–30, 35–38
human immunodeficiency virus (HIV), 15, 38–39
Human Rights Campaign
  abuse of drugs and alcohol by LGBTQ youth, 30
  basic information about, 69–70
  murders of transgender individuals (2013–2017), 49
  murders of transgender women of color, 49
  percentage harassed, assaulted, and bullied in school, 22
Human Rights Watch, 60

IBM, 63
internet, bullying on, 27, 36
intersex, defined, 12
Iran, executions of homosexuals in, 47

Jay-Z, 63
Justice Department, 41, 57

Katsas, Gregory, 58–59

Lady Gaga, 63
Lambda Legal, 58–59
Latin America, LGBTQ as victims of fatal hate crimes in, 47
laws
  federal proposed, 55
  morality legislated by, 8
  state and city
    banning conversion therapy, 28
    gay/trans panic defense banned, 50
    granting religious exemption to anti-discrimination laws, 59–60
    introduction of anti-LGBTQ, 54–55
    as only protection against discrimination, 7
    preventing anti-discrimination, 54
    prohibiting discrimination, 14–15, 52, 54
    sanctioning discrimination, 54
Levy, Diane K., 35
LGBTQ, meaning of term, 5
LGBTQ Center of Southern Nevada, 46
LGBTQ individuals, basic facts about, 5, **6**

Maril, Robin, 44
Massachusetts, 17
mass violence, 50–53, **52**
Masterpiece Cakeshop (Colorado), 60–62, **62**
McConnell, Mitch, 55, **56**
McGowan, Sharon, 59
Menashi, Steven, 59
mental health
  illnesses suffered, **29**, 30
  Pride Month activities and, **45**, 64
  stress of hiding sexual orientation, 35
  suicide, 30–31
mental illness, homosexuality as, 9
Michigan, 60
military
  homosexuals in
    banned or discharged if discovered, 9–10
    Clinton and, 16, 19

75

Obama and, 19
　　Trump and, 19
　transgender individuals in, 19, 57
Milk, Harvey, 14
millennials, number of LGBTQ, 5
Mississippi, 60
Missouri, 54
morality, homosexuals as threat to, 9–10
Moscone, George, 14
Movement Advancement Project, 41, 42

National Center for Transgender Equality
　basic information about, 70
　evictions of transgender individuals, 37
　sexual assaults of transgender prison inmates, 42
National Coalition for the Homeless, 30
National Public Radio (NPR)
　health care in rural areas for LGBTQ individuals, 39
　percentage of LGBTQ individuals closeted at work, 34
　percentage of LGBTQ individuals experiencing housing discrimination, 35
national security threats, homosexuals as, 10–11
Newton, David E., 31
New York City Anti-Violence Project, 46–47
nonbinary, defined, 12
North Carolina, 54
North Dakota, 60

Obama, Barack
　homosexuals in military and, 19
　pro-LGBTQ policies enacted, 56
　on Pulse nightclub shootings, 53
offensive comments, unintentional, 24
online bullying, 27, 36
Oregon, 14
Orlando, Florida, mass shooting in, 51–52, **52**, 53

Page, Ellen, 63

pansexual, defined, 12
Paris, Nathan, 47
Parsons, Jim, 63
Pediatrics (journal), 26, 30
people of color, LGBTQ, 39–41, **40**, 49
Perkins, Ralph, 52–53
Pew Research Center, 55
PFLAG
　basic information about, 70
　harassment of LGBTQ youth at school, 21
　services provided for LGBTQ youth, 64
Pine, Seymour, 13
Pink, 63
Pitt, Brad, 63
Pride Month activities, **45**, 64
public opinion, AIDS as punishment from God, 15
Public Religion Research Institute, 15
Pulse nightclub (Orlando, Florida), 51–52, **52**, 53

queer, defined, 12

Radcliffe, Daniel, 63
rainbow items, 44–45, **45**
Rapinoe, Megan, 42, 45
Regional Information Network on Violence Against LGBTI People in Latin America and the Caribbean, 47
religion
　AIDS as punishment from God, 15
　homophobic and transphobic doctrine, 26–27
　homosexuals as sinners, 4, 9
　support for LGBTQ rights, 61
　use of First Amendment to allow discrimination based on freedom of, 59–62, **62**
　vandalism against gay-friendly churches, 46
Religious Accommodations Act (Mississippi), 60
Republican Party, 55
Rhines, Charles, 41
Riggs, Lynn, 46
Rivera, Ray, 18
Rivera, Sylvia, 13, 18, 45–46

Saenz, Richard, 50
same-sex marriage
   Defense of Marriage Act, 16, 17
   legalized in some states, 17
   Masterpiece Cakeshop case, 60–62, **62**
   political identification and support of, 55
   rights, protections, and benefits of marriage and, 18
   Supreme Court decisions, 17, 62
Sanders, Sarah Huckabee, 59
Saxe, Rose, 48
senior living facilities, 36–37
sexual orientation, hiding
   from co-religionists, 26–27
   from family, 28, 29
   government work and, 10–11
   in military, 16
   in school, 4
   stress of, 35
   in workplace, 34
sexual violence
   homeless LGBTQ youth and, 30
   against LGBTQ boys in juvenile detention facilities, 42
   against transgender prison inmates, 42
sin, homosexuality as, 4, 9
Slater, Bee Love, 50
Smith, Gwendolyn Ann, 51
sodomy laws, Supreme Court decisions about, 8
South Dakota, 54, 60
Starling, Tommy, 38
Starr, Dazjuan, 43
Steward, Samuel, 11
Stonewall Inn uprising, 11, **13**, 13–14
substance abuse, 30
suicide, 30–31
Swift, Taylor, 63

Tennessee, 54
terminology, 12
Texas, 55, 60
Thorn, Bella, 63
Timberlake, Justin, 63
Transgender Day of Remembrance, 51
transgender individuals
   denied gender-neutral bathrooms and changing rooms, 25–26, 57
   hate crimes against, 44
   in military, 19, 57
   people of color, **40**, 40 41
   in prisons, 41, 57
   in schools, 57
   sexual assaults against, 25–26, 42
   sexual orientations of, 6
   as targets of health care discrimination, 38, 42
   as targets of housing discrimination, 37
   as targets of inadequate health care, 39, 57
   Trump administration and workplace discrimination against, 57–58
   usage of preferred pronoun, 24
   women as victims of assaults, 49–50
transphobia, definition of, 7
Trevor Project, 30–31, 70
True Colors, 30
Truman, Harry, 10–11
Trump, Donald
   anti-discrimination bill and, 55
   anti-LGBTQ policies enacted by, 57
   appointment of judges with history of anti-LGBTQ bias, 58–59
   court briefs supporting workplace discrimination against transgender individuals filed by, 57–58
   homosexuals in military and, 19
   use of First Amendment for religious exemption policies, 59

University of Connecticut, percentage of harassed, assaulted, and bullied in school, 22
University of Texas at Austin, 36
US Constitution, First Amendment, 59–62
US Supreme Court
   cases concerning workplace discrimination involving LGBTQ individuals, 33
   death sentence for gay man case, 41
   religious exemption case, 61

    same-sex marriage decisions, 17
    sodomy law decisions, 8

vandalism against LGBTQ individuals, 44–46
Vandyke, Lawrence, 58
Vanguard Award (GLAAD), 63
Verlander, Justin, 63
violence. *See* assaults
Virginia, 60
Vox (website), 41

Wagner-Martin, Erika, 28
Wagner-Martin, Jenn, 21
Washington, Kerry, 63
Whit, Salem, 23
Wicker, Randy, 18
Williams Institute, 6, 32
Winkler, Ely, 27
Winslow, Shirley, 18–19
Woodward, Samuel, 47, **48**
workplace discrimination
    AIDS and, 16
    bullying in, 33–35
    fired for homosexuality, 18
    homosexuals banned from working for federal government or contractors connected to, 11
    percentage reporting, 32
    state laws prohibiting laws preventing, 54

Trump administration and workplace discrimination against transgender individuals, 57–58
See also military

youth
    adoption and foster care denied to LGBTQ individuals, 60
    college housing, 36
    of color as targets of police, 39–40, **40**
    education of
        attitude and actions of teachers, 23, **25**
        Born This Way Foundation and, 63
        clubs at school, 23
        harassment, assaults, and bullying in school, 4, 20–23, **22**
        PFLAG services, 64
        school policies, 23–26
        state laws prohibiting schools from protecting LGBTQ students from bullying, 54
    homeless, 29–30, 63
    mental health of, **29**, 30
    organizations providing services for, 63, 64, 69–70
    sexual harassment of and violence against, 27, 30, 42
    suicide and, 30–31

PICTURE CREDITS

Cover: Sam Wordley/Shutterstock.com

 6: Maury Aaseng
10: oneinchpunch/Shutterstock.com
13: Massimo Salesi/Shutterstock.com
17: Joseph Sohm/Shutterstock.com
22: Creative Images/Shutterstock.com
25: Monkey Business Images/Shutterstock.com
29: Zack Frank/Shutterstock.com
34: fizkes/Shutterstock.com
37: CREATISTA/Shutterstock.com
40: AJR_photo/Shutterstock.com
45: Mindstorm/Shutterstock.com
48: Paul Bersebach/ZUMA Press/Newscom
52: John Arehart/Shutterstock.com
56: Christopher Halloran/Shutterstock.com
58: JStone/Shutterstock.com
62: Jerome460/Shutterstock.com

ABOUT THE AUTHOR

Barbara Sheen is the author of 106 books for young people. She lives in New Mexico with her family. In her spare time, she likes to swim, garden, cook, walk, and read.